I0545961

An Important Note:

These stories are meant to entertain.

Some channel the laughing Crypt Keeper, while others are more serious. I mean to offend no one, so please know these stories fall into the speculative and horror genres.

If you have a squeamish disposition or are easily triggered, these stories may not be right for you.

If you decide to read them, however, there are some trigger warnings.

Some of the stories deal with implied domestic violence and neglect, including Creevy's Trees, Secret Santa Helper, Yule Log, Early Daddy Day, Valentine's Day Toast.

Some are violent or bloody, including Buback, Baby New Year, Wendigo Wood.

Some are just silly.

All are written with the sole hope
of entertaining you, the reader.

Nightmares

on

Holiday

Kerry E.B. Black

Nightmares on Holiday
A collection of short holiday scares
Written by Kerry E.B. Black

The stories in this collection are works of fiction. Names, characters, organizations, places, events, and incidents are either products of the author's imagination or are used fictitiously. Any resemblance to actual persons, living, dead, or undead, or actual events is purely coincidental.

Text copyright. All rights reserved.
No part of this book may be reproduced or stored in a retrieval system or transmitted in any form or by any means, electronic, mechanical, photocopying, recording, or otherwise, without the express written permission of the publisher or author.

Published by Tree Shadow Press

Tree Shadow Press

ISBN: 978-1-948894-39-5

Cover art by Christopher Blickenderfer
of American Tattoo, Verona, PA

Printed in the United States of America

*Dedicated to all who celebrate
the wonder of each and every day -
especially those who make
even the most nightmarish times
into a holiday!
Cheers!*

Table of Contents:

Foreword

Everyone deserves a holiday, even Nightmares. Lucky are those who make every day an opportunity for a celebration. In this collection of my short stories, however, you'll explore a year of some darkness. Mount a Nightmare. I've saddled them, and they're ready to take you through holidays better enjoyed on the page, beginning with the bloody birth of Baby New Year.

You'll notice not every holiday is represented. That's not because I don't have stories for them. No, it's that this collection has grown a bit wide in the middle, and I don't want its size to overwhelm anyone. You see, at heart, I'm a bit of a minimalist, but I do love a good celebration.

Of course, Halloween, when the cooler air brings a desire to face fears with an indomitable spirit, inspires me. Like popcorn being popped for candied treats, my thoughts bounced from happy memory to terrified expectation. My imagination runs amuck, like neighborhood kids armed with T.P. and silly string on Devil's Night. I can only hope my offering's worthy of the heady delight of my favorite season!

And Christmas, which is ALSO my favorite season, with its joyous goodwill, the spirit of giving, and beautiful songs, finds itself in more than one slippery situation. And yes, I sang along as I wrote these little delights. Perhaps you'll learn more on that at the end of this volume.

Until then, enjoy your ride!

Baby New Year

The infant wailed, venting his rage against vulnerability. Hunger grumbled in his stomach like an angry bear, yet no one brought food. He watched through his balled-up fists and kicking feet as an old man wearing tattered gray robes, long, snowy hair, and a wizard-like mustache and beard that fell to his waist tottered by, leaning heavily on a gnarled cane. He settled with a groan into a rocking chair and stared with dripping eyes at a clock glowing large as a full super moon.

The baby redoubled his volume, filling the screeches with a strongly implied, "Get me some food right now, old man!"

Whether because the old man was deaf or apathetic toward the infant, neither the old man nor anyone else brought food. The baby cried on, face red with temper.

The clock ticked closer to the anticipated hour. Disembodied voices began a countdown.

The old man struggled to his feet, back hunched, feet shuffling. He reclaimed his cane and ambled to the carved wooden cradle and its unhappy resident. The baby hiccupped and sniffed, studying the old man smiling with a mouthful of rotten teeth and kind cataract-coated eyes. The old man lifted the baby and cradled him to his bony shoulder.

The old man's voice wavered like a warped vinyl record. "It's your turn now." He shuffled to the chair and backed into the seat with the baby. Carvings of all the events of past importance decorated the rocker, and the old man set it in motion, back and forth. He breathed a sour-scented coo over the babe as the celestial clock tolled the first chime announcing midnight.

The old man winced as the baby bit him on the collarbone. He hummed the year's most popular song as the infant chewed on his earlobe, his wrinkled cheek, the point of his shoulder. Bite by bite, the infant ingested the old man, devouring the previous year. Thereby, he acquired the knowledge of all earlier ages. Warm gore poured down the baby's throat. Not a drop could be wasted, no remembrance lost.

As Baby New Year finished his feast, the final chime of the celestial clock reverberated to the collected sighs of 'Auld Lang Sine.' Baby New Year patted his distended belly and sighed, ready to begin his year-long reign.

Wakey Waysa

Unseasonable weather woke things. Flowers in February. Moths tapping with spring-like breezes against screened windows.

Cindy's friend Waysa came to visit, but he'd changed. His hair fell to his shoulders, his dressy clothes dripped mud, and he smelled.

Cindy asked him to go back to sleep, but he wanted to play in the sunshine.

"Come outside," he pleaded, smiling.

She ignored worms falling from his mouth.

Valentine's Toast

Cleo spooned raspberry puree into a champagne flute, enjoying the pinking of the alcohol as she lifted it to her lips for the only Valentine's kiss she'd receive. The bubbles tickled her nose as she swallowed, but no mirth filled her soul.

Hers was a lonely heart, isolated in a country home far from her family and friends. She'd moved to the northern-most tip of the Mason-Dixon line as a new bride almost six years before.

Six years. Her marriage had not even reached the itchy seven years of that Marilyn Monroe movie. Heck, it almost didn't make it past the honeymoon.

Her heart plunged, leaden, as she remembered their first night in the honeymoon suite. She'd trembled with anticipation, dressed in a sheer white nightie. He barely noticed. He turned sports on the television.

When they finally had sex for the first time, he plunged into her with the gentleness of a lion devouring prey. She

4

assumed it hurt her because it was her first time. After, he rolled over and snored, heedless of her disquiet.

In the morning, she woke to find him, curly-haired head in trembling hands, telling her, "This was a mistake."

Her lip quivered. "A mistake?"

He glowered but said nothing.

Heat rose along her collar bone and in her face. She couldn't make eye contact as she whispered, "Is it because of last night? When we made love?" She could barely breathe, but she pushed the words through her constricted esophagus, "I think I'll get better at it with practice."

He scoffed. "That's not it."

"What is it, then? What's wrong?" When he said nothing more, she'd rubbed his back to reassure him. "Maybe you're just nervous. Jitters are normal."

"You're not listening to me." His brow hung low as storm clouds. "Why did we do this?"

She had swallowed around another lump of worry and hurt. She whispered, filled with doubt, "Because we love each other."

They'd certainly not rushed into anything. They'd dated five years before he'd asked for her hand, and they waited two additional years before they'd married. He'd known of her virginity and her desire to wait until matrimony to divest herself of it. Throughout their courtship, he'd always been a gentleman.

'Or at least I love you,' she'd thought.

"I'm taking a walk to clear my head." He'd left her there in the honeymoon suite, alone with her inner agony, for over an hour before returning with apologies and a bottle of wine.

Worry lines overshadowed her tentative smile then, but she chose to forget the unpleasantness and move forward.

In truth, she spent most of their marriage forgiving such outbursts, choosing to forget them and remain optimistic. With enough love, any relationship would succeed, even with only one source for the emotion.

She'd made herself unimportant in the marriage, not much more than a caregiver and a maid. Ignoring her hurt feelings changed nothing in her relationship. No amount of patience impacted the situation.

John hadn't touched her in months. Her skin yearned for caresses. Her heart hammered disappointment, and each night, she silently cried with frustration.

He spent his time on social media in chat rooms. He planned outings for himself and his friends. Her involvement amounted to the duties of camp follower, a person to clean their messes and prepare their meals. The guests offered more appreciation than John.

Cleo turned the drink in her hands. Within the effervescent globe of her goblet, Cleo foresaw a lonely future unless she made a drastic change.

She downed the last of it, and with it, determined a new direction for her life, one without the expectation of a partner.

The front door burst open, and with it, John rushed in, boisterous as ever. His presence filled the foyer as he kicked off muddy shoes, splattering muck onto the walls. "What's for dinner? I'm starved."

Cleo rinsed her goblet and smiled, recognizing an ease in her once restricted breathing. She leaned in the doorframe in the sultry manner of Hollywood vamps of the '40's.

He glanced in her direction, eyebrows low. "Dinner?"

"It's Valentine's Day. Did you forget?"

His face opened, almost childlike with eyebrows raised, eyes and mouth wide. "Valentine's Day? We don't care about that stuff. A bogus holiday made by card companies. Right?"

"No." She turned her back on him, returning to the breakfast counter. "You might not care about it, but I looked forward to it. Foolishly." She glanced over her shoulder at his surprise. "But I see we've no plans to celebrate."

"Sorry, Babe." He never used her name unless in anger. "I didn't think it was a big deal. You always said you hated made up holidays."

"I never said that."

"Yes, you did. Many times. Right here in this room." He pointed to the tiled flooring, as though it held a record, the way he often did to confuse her.

Instead of arguing, she shrugged. "What do you want for dinner?"

A small victory smile darted across his lips. "Didn't you make anything?"

"Nope."

He allowed storm clouds of discontent to gather again on his brow. "It'll be Hell trying to find a place without reservations today." His voice lowered to an annoyed growl. "I guess we could order pizza."

"We" in his estimation meant "She," with him equally credited for his good ideas and sense.

"I'll make a salad instead." Before he could complain, she opened the fridge and removed fruits and vegetables and began to chop.

He articulated a surprised "Uh?" which she ignored.

"What about a pizza?"

She shrugged. "If you want one, order it." She popped a cucumber slice into her mouth. "I'm making a salad."

"But I don't know where to order it from. I mean, where do you hide the menus?"

She motioned with her chin toward a folder beside the food processor. "In that folder."

His incredulity transformed into anger. "I don't know where to order it." He tossed the folder onto the counter with a huff. "You order it."

"I'm making a salad. If you want a pizza, order one."

He loomed over her. "What's going on?"

She glanced up to meet his stormy eyes, strangely no longer cowed by his distress. "I want a salad, so I'm making one. You want a pizza, so you should order one." She rinsed a tomato.

"Is this because I didn't get you overpriced flowers? This is stupid." He slapped the folder holding the menus and his phone onto the counter beside the salad bowl. "Just order the pizza. I'm getting a shower." He stalked out of the room, leaving a cloud of unstated resentment in his wake.

She retrieved his phone.

"He wants a pizza," she thought, shaking her head. "Fine. I'll make him a pizza."

She typed a message, sweet and contrite, and pressed send. Her phone 'binged' its receipt.

She sliced French Bread and slathered sauce from a jar over it. She sprinkled dried oregano, garlic powder, and basil atop, then poured on shredded provolone. With the parmesan and before the pepperoni slices, she powdered and added a handful of his pills, tossing in several over-the-counter pain relievers for good measure. Couched in so many strong flavors, she imagined their inclusion would be missed.

She popped it in the oven to bake before she finished her salad.

Raspberries in her glass turned another flute of champagne a lovely pink color. She grabbed her phone, opened her messages and read the sweet Valentine's Day text she'd composed and sent herself from her husband's phone. With enough self-pity and an abundance of aggrandizing, anyone reading it would think her husband might be a bit suicidal.

The oven timer sounded, just in time for his indignant return, hair dripping from his shower onto the hardwood. Before he could complain about his perceived maltreatment, she plated the homemade pizza and handed it to him.

He took it into their living room and turned on the television to a show she disliked.

As he tucked in, she raised her glass. "To Valentine's Day."

Senator's Son

"Beware the Ides of March."

Shakespeare made famous the advice of dreamers and soothsayers to Julius Caesar, but the emperor ignored their warnings. So, senators and trusted friends murdered the emperor on the foretold day. *Et tut, Brute?* Even you, friend? Ancient history.

Now, curating objects suspected of belonging to the one-time emperor made Genevra McBride anxious. Especially on the fifteenth of March, the Ides. Her anxiety-ridden heart threatened to explode within her.

Panic attack. She forced herself to inhale, counting to ten. *Damn.* She held the breath for a count of five before she exhaled to another count of ten. In and out, controlled, until her body relaxed.

Her colleagues mocked the concerns she presented, but Genevra felt compelled to warn the owners of the ancient Roman pieces to be displayed.

Three men brought the objects with them from their homes in Italy, loaning the collection for a brief time. These men proudly proclaimed their heritage, boasting direct bloodlines from the senators of yore, perhaps the very ones who had turned their steel against the famous Roman emperor, Julius Caesar.

"Please listen to me." She strained her neck looking at the donors. "There is something important in this paperwork, and it bears closer consideration."

They chortled. In thickly accented English, they scoffed. "Perhaps you aren't cut out for this work, my dear?"

Annoyance overrode her manners. "I most certainly am cut out for this. My training far exceeds your own," she snapped.

The three men sniggered behind their mustaches. They spoke to each other in Italian, forgetting her fluency.

"The strain is too great for her excitable mind." Damiano shook his head.

Vincenzo nodded. "Women don't belong in the workplace."

"Americans have different standards, obviously," added Guiseppi.

Genevra cleared her throat, heat burning her cheeks. "Obviously, Americans have different standards. We value ingenuity more than paternity," she sniped in Italian. "However, I earned my post through years of hard work, not pretentious genealogies."

Two of the men puffed out their chests.

"Now see here," Damiano began.

"How dare you? These objects belong to our families," Vincenzo spoke over Damiano.

The third gentleman, Guiseppi, crossed his arms over his chest, smiled, and observed.

"How did your families come to possess these things?" Genevra asked. "Willed from deceased ancestors, right? Directly from the death of others. And everyone has heard of Caesar's curse." She tapped her black leather pump with agitation. "I'm here to tell you, there may be something to it."

Damiano twirled the end of his mustache, frowning.

Vincenzo recoiled, as though wounded and ready to strike.

Guiseppi leaned his suit-clad bottom against the director's desk. His lips twitched, as though he struggled to keep his emotions at bay.

She flipped her hair over her shoulder, indignant. "The problem arises with research. Everyone who has handled this collection has run afoul of untimely tragedy."

The men all raised their eyebrows but remained silent.

"Honestly! Look at these records. And always on this auspicious day." She pointed to a series of folders filled with curator notes and personal comments.

Vincenzo scoffed. "You do realize the Ides was a celebration day, to mark the beginning of a new calendar year."

"And," Damiano said, "these items have been displayed since the 1800s."

"I know, of course. But you must admit that the Ides of March is an important anniversary for the original owners, right?" She motioned toward the folders again. "These notes. It's all here, if you would only take the time to read them, from the earliest displays to the present day." She jabbed a manicured finger at the stacks of paper. "With each showing, there are tragic consequences, and always on this date."

"Miss," Damiano glared. "Your museum is paying to display our items, yet now you don't want to."

"That's not it at all." She opened an old ledger and pointed. "Every member of the founding exhibition died of mysterious causes. On the same day."

Vincenzo scoffed. "Wasn't there a carriage accident?"

Damiano said, "And they were old men, no? Old men die."

"No, listen to me. We aren't talking only about old men. We're talking about people in the prime of their lives experiencing heart attacks, strokes, or committing suicide. One drowned. Another was electrocuted." She opened a second folder. "The display of these objects is always marred. Curators, assistants, staff die." She looked at them all. "Even owners."

The men chuckled, but Vincenzo openly laughed. "Everybody dies."

Her mouth dropped open. "But statistically, not on the same day." She jabbed her finger at the records. "It's all here. When these objects are grouped together and displayed at this time of the year, those associated with the display mysteriously die."

Guiseppi stepped beside Genevra and picked up a file. "These are only the records from the times the objects were displayed publicly." He allowed the file to drop onto the others. "The objects have belonged in personal collections for thousands of years before that. Surely you don't think mere artifacts hold a curse."

She licked her lips. "I spoke with your Grandmother." She turned to Damiano. "And your Great Aunt Maria." A nod to Vincenzo. "Your Uncle Sal. They all told me the family stories. They believe these items are cursed. They're worried for you."

Vincenzo threw his hands up in the air and muttered in Italian. Damiano's nostrils flared. "Nobody really believes in curses these days, except superstitious old fools, which we're not."

She sighed. "That may well be, but gentlemen, it will not hurt you to look at the information found in these folders."

Guiseppi scrutinized her face.

"Enough nonsense. You need to calm yourself, Ms. McBride. You surely do not expect us to take any of this seriously?" Vincenzo's deep voice rumbled with reproach.

Domiano nodded. "Exactly. And where exactly is your boss? He should be here, hearing this." He waved a dismissive hand. "We're leaving. Dinner awaits." He and Vincenzo turned at the archive door. "Coming, Guiseppi?"

Guiseppi waved them on.

Their eyes grew wide. "For real?" They laughed and shook their heads.

Genevra and Guiseppi watched them climb into a called car.

Defeat and humiliation dulled Genevra's voice. "Aren't you leaving, too?" She studied the vibrant blue inset tiles along the corridor's marble outer edge.

"No."

She looked up at him. "Why not? Surely you don't buy into the crazy American woman's wacky concern."

"Buy into? I already own an interest in a good portion of the displayed objects."

'Oh," she giggled. "I'm sorry. By 'buy into,' I mean subscribe. Believe."

"That? Well," he lifted his hands and dropped them again. "No. I don't."

She gaped. "Then why are you still here?"

"Do you mind my presence?" He laughed at her blush and stood a little closer. He towered over her diminutive frame.

"Dang," she thought, "he sure smells good." She cleared her throat and stepped back, integrating professionalism into her voice. "Of course not. It's just after everything that was said, I assumed…"

He interrupted. "Believe me. I will catch Heck for staying. They will tease me, saying I only want to get into your panties." His gaze swept over her.

Her pulse raced, and she licked her lips. She sputtered, "Really, sir, I'm an employee of an esteemed museum…"

He continued. "They would only partially be correct. He stepped closer, his expensive leather shoes squeaking. "Of course, I want to sleep with you." He cupped her chin to force her gaze up. His eyes shone dark and wide. "But I also would be a fool to ignore the research of an esteemed scholar. Even if the findings are flawed, I should be interested in discerning what you discovered."

Her skin felt aflame where his touch had lingered. "Well, then," She turned to the research to collect her thoughts. She straightened her sensible clothes and cleared her throat. Self-conscious, she rubbed beneath her chin, surprised by the lingering reaction to his touch. "You see in these oldest notes, there is some question of the true ownership of these artifacts. It's suspected they may have belonged to Julius Caesar himself, that when he was assassinated outside of Pompey's theatre in 44 B.C.E., his possessions were seized by his executioners."

"Liberators."

"Excuse me?"

"They called themselves liberators. They didn't think of their actions as murder but as a necessity." He stood tall. "After all, Caesar declared himself not only king but also a god."

She opened her mouth to argue, but instead shook her head and continued. "Of course. Liberators, though they weren't terribly sporting. There were more than sixty of them, you know, ambushing one man." She blinked up at him. "You and your companions claim to be somehow related to them, the liberators, right?"

"As well you know. We presented credentials." He puffed his chest out and nodded. "Those are the family legends you speak about. Our goods were dated by scholars more lettered than yourself."

She concealed a small smile behind her hand as she pretended to wipe her nose.

His eyebrows drew close over narrowed eyes. "Something funny?"

"Of course not. The objects are undoubtedly authenticated. Your family stories seem plausible. The question of original ownership is what remains unanswered."

"Right. Well show me your evidence."

They flipped through pages with rustles like ibis wings.

He shrugged. "What do you suppose this means?"

She considered the papers. "That we should be careful, just for today. Delay putting the items together on the Ides. That's all."

He chuckled, a deep rumble in his throat thick with five o'clock shadow. "I'm not completely convinced, but I'll talk to the others." His eyes bored into hers. "For a price."

Confusion played across her features. "Price?"

"A reasonable price for listening to your crazy, American woman ideas. After all, I will be enduring a lot of teasing because of you."

She crossed her arms before her chest, muscles tense. "Oh?"

He leaned close and whispered into her hair, "The price is a kiss."

She gasped and pushed him away. *Dang, he's cute*, she thought, but with mock indignation, she said, "Flirt much?"

"Can't blame a man for trying." He shrugged and sighed. "I'll call a car, then, and keep my dejected lips to myself."

Something reckless, something long tethered snapped within her, and she stood on tiptoes and kissed his cheek.

His mouth dropped open.

"Thank you for listening. I know that you don't necessarily believe, but really, is it worth the chance?"

He flashed a brilliant, toothy smile and nodded. They lingered a moment, both leaning toward the other, before he turned and headed for the exit. He whistled a jaunty tune she didn't recognize as he left.

Her mind whirled. "I can't believe I kissed him. I kissed him, and now he's leaving. Now, he's leaving, but he was leaving soon anyway, to go home to Italy, so what does it matter? Other than being unprofessional…"

She closed the research, turned off the light, and locked the archive office door while thoughts of deeper, more passionate kisses filled her imagination. As she headed for the subway and home, she hummed the tune he had whistled as he left.

"We'll be careful with the artifacts just for today and everything will be fine," she told herself. For the first time in days, she felt light-hearted. "Maybe he'll ask me to dinner before he leaves. Or I could ask him…"

Rush hour people crammed the station and boarded the trains. She stood at the silver metal bar and mused. Her stop came, and she climbed the stairs to street level. Before she reached her destination, her cell phone rang.

"Genevra?" Guiseppi's deep voice shook, the Italian accent thicker.

"Are you okay?"

"No. The police are on the way. Something - happened to Vincenzo and Damiano."

"What? What happened?"

"I don't know." After a weighted silence, he asked in a quiet voice, "Will you please come?"

"Of course. I'll meet you at the hotel."

She turned and dashed back into the subway, increasingly uncomfortable with but grateful for the crowd. She made her way through the turn stall to the subway, but the hairs on the back of her neck raised.

"Am I being followed?" Crowds gathered. "Safety in numbers," she muttered while acknowledging, "but crowds can conceal a pursuer."

She licked her chapping lips and hugged her purse closer to her chest. "Paranoia is unnecessary and unproductive."

Despite her internal pep-talk, sweat trickled down her back and between her breasts. A thick, psychological bar seemed to clamp around her chest, pressing against her ribs and impeding her organs.

The crowd provided protection, in theory, but she longed to escape the boxed-in sensation of its presence. "If I need to run, I'll bump into people everywhere."

She got off at the uptown station and dashed to the hotel where the Italian artifact owners lodged. Outside the entrance, two ambulances flanked a light-flashing police car. The air cooled her sweaty skin and gave her chills. Shadows pressed toward her feet like reaching arms. She skipped from each pool of light to reach her destination.

Guiseppi stood in the lobby, dazed and pale.

Genevra ran to him. "Professionalism be damned." He locked her in an embrace which betrayed his inner quaking.

"I've given my statement to the agente. I feel sick."

"What's going on? What happened?"

"They're both dead. Apparently, they passed from heart attacks." He stared into a corner of the hotel lobby without seeing it. His voice sounded far off. "Maybe one started, which alarmed the other and made him have a heart attack, too?"

She gasped, sickened by her suspicions.

"They were in Damiano's room, having drinks like most any night. Why would they both have heart attacks? They're fairly young."

Tears built up, and a shiver of foreboding shook her.

The police handed them a card and bid them a good evening. Guiseppi nodded to them and pulled her closer.

He whispered, "Will you stay?"

Despite the growing misgivings wringing her insides, Genevra whispered, "I can't leave you alone." She swallowed around a lump in her throat. "Besides, I don't want to be alone, either."

They sat on the couch in his room, ordered room service, and turned on a television show to ignore. Neither ate when the trays arrived. They barely spoke, each lost in a private reverie. He drank two glasses of deep, red wine and poured a third.

He offered her a glass. "So, what do we do?"

She shook her head. "No, thank you." She shivered, her teeth chattering. "I don't know what to do."

He wrapped her in a hug. He quivered, too.

"Wow, it's really cold in here."

He rose from the sofa to adjust the temperature. The heat circulated with a series of clicks and moans.

"Wait." Genevra searched the room. The moans weren't from the radiator. Sulfur wafted through on a chilly breeze, and she coughed. "Where's that coming from?"

The lamplight and television flickered like a candle, casting the room in alternating gloom and a pale, bluish light.

"What's happening?" Guiseppi searched with wide, frightened eyes.

As though punched in the solar plexus, she lost her breath in a pained huff.

Guiseppi doubled over at the same moment.

A shadowy gray form appeared, misty at first. Solidity grew with each step. The moans emanated from it.

"Who? What?" Guiseppi sunk to the floor, pointing a wildly quavering finger at the apparition.

The cold intensified. Breath puffed in front of their faces like ineffective shields. The spirit drew from the dimness and became even more refined. A toga. A laurel wreath. A marked, Roman profile.

Genevra sprinted to Guiseppi and squatted, arms around him. Tears streamed from her incredulous eyes. "Please, great Caesar, we mean you no harm."

"Caesar?" Guiseppi repeated, a mantra to keep the dead at bay.

The spirit leveled an empty-socketed stare at the mention of his name.

Near hysteria she burst into giggles, as though a dam holding her sanity burst. "It's Great Caesar's Ghost!" Tears continued their flow unchecked, but she stood, shielding Guiseppi. The dinner she didn't eat threatened to be expelled, "I told you not to go out on the Ides of March."

The apparition floated before her. The eye sockets yawned like empty graves, holes with a magnetism threatening to pull her in. She whimpered, but she extended her arms, as though her skinny extremities could stop this ghost if it wanted to touch Guiseppi.

A rattling preceded a bone-touching chill. "*Can es exsisto vos*, Calpernia?" The spirit reached a largely translucent hand toward her cheek. She squeezed her eyes tight, tears pushed into rivulets along her cheeks.

With eyes closed to the terror before her, she pleaded. "Please, leave us in peace. We implore you."

Another cold breeze, this redolent of rotting leather and horse's excrement, heated iron and blood, rushed past her toward Guiseppi. Her eyes flew open, and she spun. The ghost leaned in and inhaled like a death rattle. "*Vos es non a liberatores. Vos es non a orchestra felius.*"

With those words, Caesar dissolved like a fog touched by sunlight.

They clung to each other, near hysteria, until their chills declined. Guiseppi wiped her tear with the back of his thumb, tipped her chin up, and kissed her on each cheek.

She gazed into his dark eyes and felt warm for the first time since entering the hotel room. She nestled closer to him and kissed his lips. Her heart rate increased, inspired not by terror but by desire.

"The ghost. Caesar. He called you Calpurnia. His wife."

"He said you were not a liberator, not a senator's son."

They kissed into the night, talking no more of the dangers brought by the Ides of March.

Blakulla Hjalte

Greta hopped after the children but could not keep up. She held collected sticks tight against her body with her curled left hand, but a small one slipped through. She sighed and watched it twitching on the ground. The delay sent the other kids far from her. Today they cavorted, and even at a regular pace, Greta's limp prevented her from keeping up with them.

She wobbled in a stoop and, with great care, retrieved the twig. She heard the others' laughter echo through the woods, but she could not catch up.

Darnit, she thought.

A small black cat crept from the underbrush, purring. Greta smiled at it.

"Ah, Trolleri, will you walk with me to the bonfire, my friend?"

The cat bumped its soft head against her leg brace and continued to purr.

The two progressed after the others, Greta with purpose, her furry friend distractible company. Snowdrifts melted into silver rivulets. Jewel-bright wildflowers and hearty crocus bulbs decorated with fragrance. Greta chatted to Trolleri who regarded her with bright, unblinking golden eyes.

"Tonight we set the bonfires to scare the witches away from their Blakulla. Will you come with me when I dress up, please? Momma made the best costume! I'll have rosy cheeks and a shawl! I made pictures for everyone, so maybe I can get lots of candy. Do you like candy?"

The cat meowed, teeth flashing like a glimpse of a pearl within an oyster.

"Oh, you prefer herring and salmon. I can get some for you, my friend! I bet that you'll love the anchovies in Jannson's Temptation! They're covered with cream."

When she reached Mr. Eriksson's farmyard, she deposited her collection of sticks with the pile by the laid bonfire. Mr. Eriksson nodded thanks, and Mrs. Eriksson offered her a cup of warm cider.

"Thank you for your help, Greta! Please give my regards to your momma, and I'll be happy to see you tonight."

Greta smiled her thanks. "It's going to be such fun!"

Trolleri hid in the angelica bushes during the exchange, then joined the girl when she left for home. The cat capered about the girls' irregular gate, snaking between her strides. Greta waved to neighbors sweeping out their homes, and shyly smiled at the city families opening their country dwellings for the season.

Wagtails twittered and hopped, attempting to attract mates. Squirrels chased each other's bushy tails. Her cottage hid among elderflower and loganberry bushes. Momma hung sheets to air on a wire stretched between two trees. The white material flapped like sails in the chilly spring breeze, ruffling momma's golden hair.

"Greta girl, there you are! Let's get you into your witch costume." She wrapped her long, wiry arms around her daughter. Greta breathed in her lemongrass scent. They held hands, making their way inside. Trolleri followed along, purring, and was rewarded with a saucer of cream while the two tow-heads prepared for the night's festivities.

Rosy circles accented Greta's cheeks. Her hair hid beneath a bright headscarf, a lacy shawl about her thin shoulders, and she carried a straw broom. Roasting lamb, parsnips, carrots, and onions fragranced the cabin with promises of an evening's delicious smorgasbord.

"If you grow weary from the walk, lean on the broom stick. It is sturdy, like a crutch."

The cat batted a painted boiled egg from the table with an insolent swipe of a padded front paw.

"Trolleri, bad kitty!"

"It's okay, love. Go, deliver your letters and collect your candy!" She slung over Greta's slim shoulders a long-strapped satchel containing "Glad Pask" or "Happy Easter" cards and bits of wax-wrapped caramels. She wrapped her daughter in another hug, saying, "You sure are the cutest Paskarringar ever!" They rubbed noses, then girl and cat left Momma to tidy the egg mess and complete evening preparations. Family would arrive from town as the light faded, since in Sweden, holidays were spent in the natural beauty of the country. The Eriksson's invited them to their bonfire.

They stopped at the neighbor, the Jorgenssons' blue-shuttered house first. Their family scampered among the grasses, hiding painted cardboard eggs. They smiled when Greta approached.

"Ah, a Paskarringar! Quick, get the candy!" they laughed.

Greta grinned and reached into her satchel, retrieving the spring-themed card she made for them.

"Oh, Greta, this is beautiful! Thank you, and Glad Pask to you, too!" Mrs. Jorgensson slipped candy into her satchel and reached down to scratch Trolleri's ear. "How did you train your cat to follow along?"

"I didn't. She just comes along when she wants to."

"Well, puss, you make Greta's costume authentic looking!"

They took their leave. She handed cards to all of the neighbors along the way in exchange for candy.

The Eriksson's bonfire pit was piled high with wood, ready to illuminate the night sky and confuse witches on the way to their nefarious doings at Blakulla. Greta's pulse increased when Ander Ericsson started the blaze. The muscles in his arms bunched, and Greta found breathing difficult. He was nearly twenty and, with long, dark blond locks and chiseled features, could easily advertise the benefits of healthy country life. He noticed her stare and flashed a straight-toothed smile that would put Hollywood actors to shame. She ducked her chin to her shoulder, looking for the cat, as a blush burned its way from collar bone to hairline.

She heard his hearty laugh follow as she limped after a group of disguised classmates.

"Hey," she called, breathless, "Can I walk with you?"

The three girls turned their rouged-cheek faces to her. The tallest, Kim, cocked her head to the left and made a pout. "No, you can't because you don't really walk, now do you, Hop-a-long?" She crossed her arms in front of her white-starched apron before turning on her heel and setting off at a rapid pace. "Come on, we don't want to go so slow that we miss all of the fun tonight!" The other girls shrugged and followed their friend.

Breathing rapidly with suppressed emotion, Greta swallowed an angry retort. The cat bumped its little black head against her ankle brace with a soft thud. Greta's nostrils flared, but petting the cat calmed her. "Stupid girls. It's not my fault I can't walk fast. And it is not nice to call me names."

Fireworks screamed into the sky from the Eriksson's backyard, making her and the cat jump. She laughed to dismiss her embarrassment. "Let's go! It will be dark soon."

She felt fatigued. She did not feel like wearing the Easter witch costume any longer, nor did she want to be left behind by her classmates.

"I'll eat all of the caramels that momma made for the kids from school all by myself. They aren't nice to me, anyway." She decided to take the shortcut home through the woods.

Crying, though, stopped her crunching through the decaying leaves. The cat arched its back, fur fluffed, and she hissed.

"Who's there?" Greta called.

The crying stopped, and another Paskarringar stepped from the shadows, wiping her nose on a patch-work sleeve. Greta did not recognize the girl.

"Hello! Are you lost?"

"Yes!"

Greta considered. "Come with me, then, and my momma will help you."

She sniffed. "Okay. Thank you."

The girls walked through the deepening dusk. Trolleri's eyes glowed golden as she kept watch.

Greta introduced herself.

The girl said, "I'm Inga."

"It is nice to meet you, Inga! Are you from town?"

Inga's brows knitted together, then she nodded.

Greta stopped to catch her breath. She reached into her bag and asked, "Do you have family close by?"

"My sisters should be somewhere about." She searched the smoke-streaked sky.

Trolleri hissed again and streaked ahead, an elongated velvety shadow.

"Your cat is beautiful. I would like such a friend."

"Thank you," said Greta, wondering about Trolleri's strange behavior. She did not typically hiss. When she was shy, she hid. Greta pushed off with the broom to walk the short distance home.

She looked sideways at her companion. Inga was older than Greta or her classmates, probably about twenty, with flaxen hair peeking from a red headscarf. She wore no ruddy makeup, but freckles belied a love of the sun. She had delicate features and a slight build, and she did not mind slow walking, nor did she call names or comment on Greta's braces or spastic hand.

They reached her home. Relatives enveloped Greta in familial cheer.

"Happy Easter!"

"My how lovely!"

"Did you grow a head taller since last I saw you?"

She found her momma and turned to introduce Inga, but the girl vanished in the holiday hubbub.

That's peculiar, Gretta thought.

After eating, Momma handed everyone flashlights or lanterns, and the group stumbled to the bonfire. The sooty smell reached them first, then the crackling pops and conversation. An occasional burst of light and bang announced a firework.

Greta spotted Inga illuminated by the firelight. Her uncovered hair hung in soft tangles to her waist, and her patched clothing lent an exotic, gypsy-like appearance. She touched Ander Ericsson's muscular forearm and held Greta's cat. Ander stared and grinned, chuckling at Inga's every word. The cat slept, slumped over her arm.

Greta felt breath leave her as though punched in the gut. *What's that Inga doing with Ander and Trolleri?*

She stomped heavily, thumping her way to the girl she had found crying in the woods. She ignored Kim's muttered "Hop-a-long," focused and filled with purpose.

A firework shot silver sparks whistling overhead. Greta did not start. She marched up to the strange girl and interjected herself by standing between the flirting pair.

"Hey," Ander exclaimed, but Greta left him in her shadow and focused on the girl. *Why was Trolleri slumped in her arms like a doll?* "Found your sisters yet, Inga?"

The beauty stroked the sleeping cat and smiled. "I may have found one after all."

She pointed to Trolleri. "Why do you have my cat?"

"Why, this is my cat." Her smile broadened.

People overhearing murmured. Some backed away, but others leaned in to catch the gossip. Greta looked for a friendly face. She did not know who to trust, so she raised her voice and pointed to the sleeping feline. "Whose cat is this?"

The hissing of the bonfire was the only sound for several seconds.

"Hop-a, I mean Greta, that cat probably just looks like your cat," reassured Ander.

She spun and looked at him, shook her head, then said even louder, "Trolleri is my cat. He has a white spot on his stomach."

Most of her neighbors knew Greta as a quiet, non-confrontational girl. This changed behavior alarmed them.

Mr. Eriksson said in a slow, calm voice, "Honey, what seems to be the problem?"

Momma rested a hand on his shoulder, saying, "Obviously, this girl is trying to claim my girl's pet. Let's see its stomach, please, young lady." Momma's arms reached for the limp cat. Inga's eyes glinted in the firelight, reflecting the glow the way an animal's might. She turned away with the sleeping cat.

A calm overtook her, and Greta understood. "You lost your way when the fires smoked, didn't you, Inga?"

A gasp and whispers rippled through the crowd.

Inga pressed her lips together in a thin line and narrowed her feverish eyes. "What nonsense are you spouting, hopping girl?"

Her nostrils flared, but Greta ignored the gibe. "I was nice to you. I helped you. Now give me my cat."

Inga scoured the area as though scoping out an escape. With no easy route available, she threw the cat toward Greta. "Fine, here, have your darned cat!"

Trolleri woke mid-air, paws splayed in needle-sharp claws, eyes saucer-wide with terror. When the cat hit into her chest, Greta stumbled back toward the fire.

Someone screamed. Momma rushed forward. Inga laughed and turned in a swirl of material and glistening hair.

Ander reached out and stopped Greta from falling into the flames.

Trolleri purred an apology, licking Greta's scratches. Ander shook like a marathon runner, muttering. Momma hugged her daughter and pulled her away from the fire's heat. "My baby girl, thank God you are okay."

No one saw Inga the witch again. Despite disparaging murmurs of 'superstitious country folk,' the tradition of lighting bonfires prospered with renewed urgency. Trolleri remained a prized family pet. Best of all in Greta's estimation, she earned a new, respected nickname, Hjalte, hero, and some even called her friend.

Love and Porcelain

"You're my best friend. That's why I'm hugging you. I hug what I love." Starr leaned against her smaller - and less drunk - friend, Autumn.

Autumn shifted her weight to support her friend. "Love you, too. Keep walking, though. You said you didn't feel well."

Starr froze, concern broadcasting across her features. Terror gripped Autumn. "Hold on, honey! Just a few more steps."

They plod-hurried like ungainly sack-race contestants into the bar's women's room. Autumn held Starr's hair. "Better out than in," she reassured.

Emptied, Starr clasped the cool porcelain. "I love this toilet bowl!"

"Well, you are hugging it."

Beyond My Peripheral

I've always felt him there, just beyond my peripheral, his scent of Irish moss and his touch a gentle brush against my hair. He lured me with succulent sweets, an invisible guide into the unknown. He promised I'd sup on the sinister and manage miracles.

They, those in charge, my parents, and teachers and counselors, told me to set aside delusions and focus on the tangible and real. They assured me nobody called from the recesses, that magic belonged in children's books and on Vegas stages.

So, I denied my longing for forbidden fruits and poured myself into academics. Actuary Sciences, with its promised income and employability. School in a city, with limited greenspaces, allowed me to push him from my waking thoughts, though he danced through dreams.

Nothing dislodged him from my dreams, where he whispered wonders to my hidden heart.

Tonight, though, I'm home on spring break, and drawn, unable to resist, outdoors to where wild things cower, hunkered far from his pheromones. Thick fog engulfs garden pathways, and a fairy fever settles over me. I burn, desirous of all I've denied, like I am Brigid before demoted from goddess to saint. I hum a childhood tune, one where in the white space between the inky black notes he hides.

Always out of reach, yet always there - just beyond my peripheral.

Egg Hunt

Spring breezes tickled as Briony rushed to collect bright colored eggs, but the bigger kids with their longer legs and quicker arms snatched them all. She stomped, dejected, and flounced onto the ground in a pout. Something drew her eye. She squatted, pastel skirt brushing the grass as she crab-walked under an azalea where she'd spotted an egg, deep purple with vivid red veins. Briony carefully placed it in her pink plastic basket, but it cracked, smelling rotten. "Ew," Briony complained, wrinkling her little nose. Quick as thought, pliant tentacles, deep purple with vivid red veins extended from the shell, coiled up her chubby arm, clambered over her shoulder, and snaked around her neck. It squeezed until her face turned a brilliant purple, with vivid red veins lacing her eyes.

Nobody at the egg hunt heard her strangled scream.

Expanded from the original which was published in Speculative 66

Oestra

Every season requires sacrifices, but the worst, in my opinion, is Spring.

In Spring, snow melts into silvery rivulets, turning the ground into quagmires carried about on shoes' bottoms and puppies' paws, tracked into houses, miring carpets. Landscapes become pitted with every footfall. Tender grasses squelch into the mud, buried until the sun grows in strength and can support the stalks.

Beneath the young roots, worms wriggle, swim through saturated soil to reach the surface and gasp. Grubs glut on impetuous fibers, killing before plants have the chance to leaf or green.

I see my students, eager as colts to dash across the quad, to sully the marble halls with their tracks and their energetic whoops, as though they've burst into flower with the feeble first rays of spring. They gaze with renewed awe at each other, their pheromones inflamed, like all of the animals.

Birds dip and dive, singing their pleasure with wanton abandon. Those who hibernate stretch and growl their intentions to the still-barren landscapes. Squirrels, too, make acrobatic displays in courtship of each other.

Of course, rabbits, the symbol of the season for their rapacious multiplication, scurry hither and yon, gathering intelligence for their mistress. They make perfect spies, because nobody suspects them of malice or even wit, but within their rapid hearts beat an ancient and organized network coded in leg thumps and flashed cotton tails.

A surprisingly large number of T.A.s or their mates are swollen ripe with children planted last summer, at celebrations of the longest of days. My own waddles, hand resting low on her back, a weary smile stretched across her pretty face. Always eager to please, Mari fights through fatigue to assist when it is she who should recline on silken benches, fanned, fed, and pampered, since her body mirrors the personifications of this season.

Soon, from her, life will spring.

I shiver with dread but hand her a stack of papers to grade. "No curve," I explain. She nods. There will be no slack when the stakes rise.

I recline, the window of my office open to the plunk of melting ice, a fresh perfume to cover the rot of decaying mulch thus disturbed. With each drip, time ticks toward the inevitable.

Mari winces, tenses, breathes deep, relaxes. Ten to twelve minutes apart. She doesn't think I notice, but I recognize the signs. At the end of the workday, she presents the graded papers, her margin notes inked in purple, not red like my own editing complaints. My head throbs as I thank her. Sweat slicks her temples, like icicles of worry bleeding across her face.

I hand her a packet of tea. "I couldn't help but notice. This will help speed things along, now that you've started down this path."

She hugs the pouch to her breast, eyes glinting with unshed tears. "Thank you, professor."

I puff up in an attempt to look parental. "You're welcome, Mari. Just be safe and phone me with updates. I don't expect to see you tomorrow."

For one terrible, heart-stopping moment, I thought she might hug me to her bosom, like she clung to the tea. Her gratitude almost undoes me. But she is young, fertile. She'll never understand her importance, or rather the importance of what she'll bare.

The season changes, and Spring will have the most succulent to sate her appetite.

As expected, I receive word that Mari's labors produced a girl. Her textbook homebirth would allow easy visits, though I forgot the child's name.

It's easier that way. No matter how many seasons pass, the price always weighs heavy on my soul.

My thoughts bounce through lessons and student cares and my responsibilities, because it always falls to the responsible to do what others cannot. After classes, I prepare a basket with four opaque goblets, sweet wine, creamy cheeses, and salty bread sticks, grab my exchange bag, and visit my T.A. and her new arrival.

Mari glows, wild-eyed with relief and enchanted with her babe. She blushes a "you shouldn't have" when she accepts her gift. I uncork the bottle and pour glasses for a toast.

She hesitates before saying, "One shouldn't hurt." Her partner agrees without compunction. I hide my lack of wine from them with a pantomimed pour and studied sip.

I raise the glass and nod. "To you. May you always be fruitful and happy."

New parenthood, a full belly, and strong wine wrap a blanket of exhaustion, and with their heads touching like the top bumps of a heart, momma and pop doze, snore, dream of life with their golden triangle while I orchestrate their devastation and salvation.

From my exchange bag I pull the imposter, the changeling. I strip the new human of her clothes to swath the purple and blue imposter. The changeling always arrives in the exchange bag, unbidden, on the day of the swap. The resemblance astounds, like always, a perfect imitation of its living counterpart.

I lay it in the crib alongside the slumbering couple, write a quick note of "You drifted off and all looked so peaceful, I didn't have the heart to wake you. So, I left. Congratulations again. I have the feeling your little one will make a huge difference in this world of ours. All the best," and fled before they woke.

The timing couldn't be better.

I climbed the path to the top of the hills overlooking Ol Nor-Eastern U, my workplace and home these last thirty-five years. From this vantage, the entire campus spread to the west, gray stone buildings, cobbled pathways, quaint and ordered to provide excellent educations. The fertility of the students' minds mattered as much as the fruitfulness of the surrounding farmland's harvests.

Here, however, no wicker-man need be burnt, its ashes plowed into the fields.

Here, Spring desired the tenderest morsels.

The babe slept, doubtless lulled by my steady progress to the sacred clearing. Birch trees, evergreens, thick thatches of rhododendrons and mountain laurel stood witness, ready to burst from Winter's grip. No birds twittered within the sacred circle. No little rodents scampered. Even the dormant stand of wild roses remained silent, anxious for the ceremony and its outcome. Clouds obscure overhead, conspirators.

Sacred words in the ancient tongue, lyrical as a lullaby, call them from their corners, the others cloaked in white, faces hidden within heavy hoods. I shelter behind my own, grateful for the anonymity.

I stuff the child's mouth with cotton, ignoring its thrashing. I couldn't endure its cries.

From my bag, I draw and make quick use of the sacred knife. In wide-mouthed glass jars I capture each precious drop of blood, mindful of its value. As it fills the containers, the child's jerky flailing slows, weakens, stops.

In the center of the circle, a fire burns beneath a cauldron large enough to bathe in. I surrender the still and blue child to the embrace of the softly boiling liquid within. It bops to the top, dips below, reappears, closed eyes, downy hair, perfect fingernails at the end of impossibly small fingertips. She radiates peace, harmony, and perfect love.

After all, it's a sacrifice for others that saves all, and no truer love exists.

I cap the jars and distribute them to the outstretched hands of my gloved brethren. They clutch the precious glass to their chest, much as Mari, the young mother, had accepted my small gift of tea not two full days before.

I turn from the scene before this thought can blossom into a regret, my own artifact from the activity warm against the skin of my neck. The exsanguinated baby boils, as is written in sacred books. The others will tend to the preparation of the fertilizer. Often, they grind the tiny bones to fortify the flour, but I've requested she be prepared, wired, and reassembled. The science department could use another skeleton, and an infant's might inspire greater understanding of human development.

As I meander back to my car, I open the jar's lid and marvel. Where any drops of blood I allow to fall land, swaths of pale violet bloom, tiny perfect treasures announcing the arrival of Spring.

Arbor Day Uprising

Coverage of the Arbor Day Altercation on the US Senate floor went viral worldwide. Otherwise strait-laced senators and their assistants lunged at the reporting representatives from the Bureau of Land Management, the World Wildlife Fund, and other conservation agencies - and at each other. Later press releases blamed the incident on everything from mass hysteria to a gas leak in the building.

Nobody wanted to blame the real culprits. The senators.

But that lack of accountability brought about the problem in the first place.

An impassioned plea from ecologically minded groups spurred to action when Congress proposed infringing on protected lands west of the Mississippi. Protesters marched on Washington. People from the Tribes of Native Americans demonstrated. Grass roots organizations poured money into research and hired lobbyists. Despite it all, Congress prepared to pass a bill to extract natural

45

resources from protected - and to many American Indian tribes, sacred - lands.

A "green" delegation made an eleventh-hour attempt to persuade the senators to make an ethical decision, knowing the passage of the bill meant the permanent alteration of thousands of acres of protected land. The more cynical of the conservationists, led by Dr. Annie Bright Star Guardipee, brought along a backup plan.

Dr. Guardipee knew the land spirits, knew their pain and their anger. She sat in communion with them when the government began talks of regaining control of land protected since the time of the first president Roosevelt. Her quest enlisted allies Washington DC had never faced.

Fungi spirits sent spores through the ventilation system, granting visions. While everyone on the senate floor tripped, swarms of gnats and other biting nuisances irritated skin and eyes. Squadrons of wasps unsheathed their stingers while serpents slithered from beneath benches and nipped Achilles tendons and shins.

The resulting pandemonium ended as abruptly as it began, without a trace of the offending natural assailants. When asked about it, Dr. Guardipee smiled, her face a cypher. "It seems to me the people of the United States might need to rethink their elected officials. If they couldn't conduct themselves professionally during a session of Congress, why should they be trusted to make important decisions?"

An eager reporter thrust a microphone beneath Dr. Guardipee's nose. "What do you think will happen if senators continue to push the contested bill?"

Dr. Guardipee removed her eyeglasses and stared into the camera. "I imagine nature has a lot to say on the matter and will make Herself known." As Dr. Guardipee turned from the reporter, a haunting, disembodied voice added, "Perhaps even in increasingly aggressive ways."

Thunder rumbled over Washington D.C. with cracks of lightning illuminating the dark skies, the perfect punctuation to an important message.

Mama Day

She remembered the conception - sort of. A night of drinking and a handsome stranger in a curtained, four poster bed better suited for Tudor England than Pittsburgh's North Side, but the B&B was clean, and he was paying.

She used protection, but still, this thing took root in her womb. It squirmed inside her, pushing aside organs and pressing against her spine, taking all the nutrients, a perfect parasite. Because she didn't believe the signs at first, she didn't seek medical attention. She lost a tooth and clumps of hair. She forced horse pills smelling of vanilla and tasting of blood through her nauseated lips.

When the contractions came, she vomited and messed her pants and cursed her night of pain and passion with a stranger in a curtained four poster bed. Alone in the delivery room, she screeched and pushed and bit a wooden rod until it tore from her with a gush of blood and amniotic fluid and a shriek akin to diving hawks.

They cleaned her womb's invader and set him at her breast where he gnawed to feed, looking up with Rosemary's Baby's Eyes.

Early Daddy Day

He'd had it. The kid ran the house. All it had to do was open his toothless mouth, and the world dropped everything to tend it.

Their mama didn't even bother to clean up anymore. She'd grown fat and lazy, with stretch marks and a c-section scar that reminded him of seeing her insides outside of her, laying on her distended stomach, slimy with gore, when the kid was born.

He couldn't look at her without remembering the gush of foul-smelling, murky mess that flooded his Challenger's front passenger seat. Water breaking, his ass, unless the water in question was a rotting pond.

She yelled from the bathroom with a whiney voice, "Hon, please pick up the baby while I finish my Sitz bath."

He'd pick up the baby, all right. The thing's face purpled with impotent rage, tiny fists flailing, kicking feet freed from a soft, new blanket. It weighed less than seven pounds, seven pounds of poop and piss and vomit. All it would take is one slip, one "oops, I dropped it!" and he'd reclaim solidarity over his house again.

Oh, Canada Day

July begins with a mad maple blast
Celebrating Canada, present and past.
Mounties uniformed march upon the scene
Making many manic Mademoiselles scream.
Dripping in patriotism,
Draped in white and red.
Among them frolic ghosts
Unaware they are dead.
Picnics, proclamations, citizenship,
Spectated by specters strolling through a rip
In the land of afterlife wishing to stay.
Canadian hospitality's famous, eh?

Three Cheers for the Red, White, and Boom

Maggie clutched Trevor's hand, ignoring the sweat that slicked the connection. A glorious sun sparkled in the uncharacteristically blue Pittsburgh sky as the young couple weaved through the crowd to stake a spot to watch the upcoming fireworks display.

More than the excitement of a first date with the man she'd admired for two years caused her heart to bound with greater percussion than a Sousa composition. Maggie distrusted crowds and feared fireworks, had for as long as she could remember. However, when Trevor asked her to join him for the Independence Day festivities at Point State Park, she couldn't refuse.

"We should be able to see great right here. What do you think?"

A shy smile wobbled across her face. "Sure."

He folded a tattered, pale blue comforter in half and spread it atop the grass. "If you stay here, I'll get us some ices. What flavor do you like?"

She fanned her sundress skirt around her tanned legs as she took a seat and considered. "Root beer, I guess."

Trevor's gaze gobbled up the sight of her, his admiration obvious. "Good god, you're gorgeous."

She blushed hot as the July sun.

He blushed as well, ducking his head and running a hand along the back of his neck. "I like root beer, too." He stole a glance through his lush, dark lashes. "Be right back. Don't disappear."

"I'll be right here." She watched the muscles of his legs work as he snaked through the assembly toward the food carts lining the park's city side.

Crowds gathered, chattered, and broke apart around her, mostly young people near her age, but with the occasional family present as well. Maggie eyed them warily, darting glances while hoping for Trevor's return.

Her favorite Disney animated movie, *Beauty and the Beast*, taught her crowds can easily become mobs, given the right incentive.

Before too long, Trevor dropped to a graceful seat beside her, extending a red and white striped cardboard cup and spoon. "Hope they haven't melted."

She scooped a bite. "Mmm, this hits the spot."

He smiled around his own mouthful. "Nothing quite like an Italian ice on a hot day."

They filled the time until dusk with light flirting and snacks. He threaded his arm around her shoulder, asking, "Is this ok?" She nodded, bashful, and leaned against him, inhaling the mix of sunscreen and a fruity cologne.

He rested his cheek atop her head. "Good thing we got a spot. The crowd's even bigger than last year's."

"Do you think it's because there's a new company putting on the show?"

He shrugged. "I don't think anyone can top Zambelli's. They're real pros, but I guess they had a problem at their warehouses this year."

She lowered her voice. "The afternoon talk show said officials suspect sabotage."

"I heard that, too, but I doubt it. Gunpowder's pretty heavily regulated, especially here in Pennsylvania."

Inspirational, instrumental music filled the airwaves and quieted some of the crowd. A few people whooped and clapped. A magnified announcer proclaimed, "Welcome to this year's Independence Day celebration! It started in the 1770's, when some uppity colonists decided to break away from their rightful king."

A few in the crowd tittered. Maggie frowned. "That's a weirdly unpatriotic stance."

"Yeah," Trevor agreed.

A few fireworks lit the night sky, reds, blues, whites bursting in sparkles and booms. The crowd ooh'd and ahh'd. The announcer continued, "They met in secret to hatch their plot and draft their plans. A declaration. Stolen goods. Shirked responsibilities. Eventually, war, with its deaths and destruction."

Booms and flashes of color exploded overhead, punctuating the narration and the music. Small, charred bits rained on the watching crowd. The shrapnel scorched a hole in their blanket and singed Maggie's skirt. She brushed pieces from her hair, uncomfortable with the heat she met as she did so.

A large piece plunked and hissed into the fountain at the point where Pittsburgh's three rivers met. Other people in the crowd reacted with yelps or uncomfortable laughs, hops and "ouches."

Thick, gray smoke rolled from the launch points, fencing in the observers, a smoke that brought tears and coughs and quick-forming rashes on exposed skin. The murmurs from the crowd rose and drowned out the narration. Fireworks pounded the night, accompanied by mortar blasts and rising screams.

People sheltered under blankets and batted away glowing pieces with bottles, cups, and hands. Groups clumped and surged toward the exit, pushing the confused in their growing swell. They searched the sky, ignoring their feet, so they tripped over one another in their fervor to escape.

Maggie and Trevor clung to one another with the blue blanket stretched over their heads. People bumped into them, knocked them about like a trailer caught in a tornado. Trevor tried to merge with the growing gang, but Maggie tugged on his t-shirt's sleeve.

"Let's try this way," she yelled over the pandemonium.

"But the car's parked out here."

"If they get knocked over, we'll be trampled to death. If we hug the perimeter, we might stand a better chance."

"I wish we could see. This damned smoke's killing us."

Maggie hoped he wasn't speaking in hyperbole, fearful of pain radiating from her lungs and joints. "Let's get closer to the ground. Less smoke there."

"Won't we get trampled for sure then?"

"Not if we stay away from the throng."

As they hunched closer to the ground and hurried to the edge of the park, the screams turned to moans. People collapsed. Some stooped to pick up their fallen friends. Others scrambled faster, plowing through to hoped-for safety. A pigtailed child wailed beside her fallen mother, still clutching the immobile mother's hand. A fashionably bearded gent threw hip checks and elbows like an old-time footballer. More people crumpled, their knees giving way to drop them. Some stopped mid stride to cradle their heads before they, too, fell.

Maggie's vision swam, and she swayed. She faltered, but Trevor supported her. "Lean on me." His voice sounded distant. His eyes shed tears of thin blood. She swiped her own and found a slick of red along her fingertips. "What's happening?"

Trevor groaned and folded in on himself. Maggie thudded to a kneel beside him. "Please, get up," she cried. "I can't carry you."

"Sorry, love. I don't think I can walk further."

"Then let's crawl." Like toddlers they scurried on hands and knees, sucking the cooler air close to the trampled park grass. By inches they continued as the fireworks' grand finale gobbled up the darkness.

Before the final, resounding boom, emergency workers slipped gas masks over their faces and dragged them to the nearby hotel with other survivors of the Independence Day attack.

Stars in the Sand

The Caribbean lapped the sandy shore, spitting shells and wriggling creatures in its wake while it reached to consume her toes. Bea gaped at the moonbeams trapped within the ocean's waves, though not trapped at all. Unlike her Rodrick, the moonbeams danced along the salted spray, never truly held captive. The oceanic jailor couldn't hold the lusty moon and was, in fact, another captive of the lunar caprice. After all, the moon controlled the tides.

Bea had met Rodrick years ago at a concert along this very beach. His metal band ripped merciless chords and screamed feedback until her ears rang with remembrance. He stared from the spotlight into a crowd of hundreds and noticed only her. His bass slung low, he inched toward the edge of the stage and reached for her hand. Bemused, she stretched her fingers and stood on tiptoes, until her nails brushed the calloused tips of his. When he sidled up to the microphone, flipping his thick dreads over his shoulder, he sang eternal love to her until she felt her heart leave its safety and lodge in his leather-clad chest.

He traveled with the band, so they didn't have much actual time together. Theirs were stolen moments. Her life on a small island kept dating options to a minimum, even if her loyalty didn't already rest at his feet. The couple spoke on the telephone and texted every day, though, and Bea never doubted Rodrick's affections. "You're like a nova, lighting my way home. With you on the beach, I'll never get lost."

She hugged her phone to her chest, a girlish squeal, and a twirl of pale skirts as she spun with bliss. "I'm his home!"

Within a year, they married. They honeymooned in the pure white sands of her island in remembrance of their meeting under the full moon when the sea sang along with the band. No need to leave when she already lived in paradise, he'd reasoned, dismissing her shy hints at "Anywhere but here, please. I've never seen the world beyond these shores."

He ran a finger along the hollow of her cheek and smiled. "Hush. This is perfect. Don't spoil it." He kissed her, long and deep, until her thoughts muddled. "Besides, now you're mine."

She leaned into his shoulder. "And you're mine."

A cuffing laugh shook her head from its comfort. "I'm yours." Sarcasm glutted the words, but Bea dismissed her hurt with the conviction she must have misread his intentions.

After they hastily consummated their union, he retired to the balcony of their honeymoon suite and stared at the star-strewn sky. She shivered into a hotel robe and brought its match to her husband. He ignored the robe but slipped an arm around her waist.

She winced. "Sorry. I'm a bit sore." In answer to his questioning gaze, she blushed and whispered, "You were a bit rough."

He snorted. "Just making it memorable for you."

She pulled the robe tighter about her, as though she could thereby insulate herself from her growing concerns.

Her stomach clenched as their relationship grew in dysfunction and abuse. She began to pray for his absence, but the band broke up, and he had no motivation to pursue a different career.

They rented a little bungalow not far from Grace Beach where he played his guitar for tourists and locals, and they filled his case with castoff cash. His tempers grew as the moon swelled, and he'd often storm out with a slammed screened door. Bea curled on the bed and dreaded his return. When the ocean's breeze whispered through the palm fronds like serpentine warnings, he remained away from her until the horizon swallowed the full moon and spat out a blazing sun. When he returned those mornings, his clothes stunk of brine and bore lipstick-red patches in damning splotches she dared not ask about.

When he harried her to distraction, she suggested she find work herself.

"I don't want you to take a job," he snarled at her. "Your job is taking care of me."

She redoubled her attentions at home, sharing special favors with the hope he'd be pleased and stop being so changeable. One minute, she recognized the romantic who won her, but the next, she kept her head low to avoid attracting the lightning of his anger.

After she'd spent a day preparing a sweet potato curry the way she thought he liked, he slapped the plate from her hand.

He towered over her, aggression marring his otherwise beautiful features. "Are you trying to starve me? I need meat."

She stooped to clean the ruined meal, trembling. With the rejected dinner in hand, she steeled herself, emboldened. "You liked this when we ordered it at the Del Mar on our honeymoon. That's why I made it."

Again, he loomed over her, hulking menace until she cowered. "Well, today I need meat." He pulled his lips back to expose abnormally pointed teeth.

She recoiled, hands covering her horrified expression.

His entire visage had changed. Chiseled jaw elongated. Whiskers thickened. Even his dreadlocks puffed about his face, like raised hackles, forming an ebony mane that framed his anger. Worst of all, his eyes bulged, their pupils enlarged until only slim bands of sunken color encircled them while the whites jutted unnaturally.

She backed into the bungalow wall, aware of the fragility of the structure. If so minded, a tropical storm could whirl the thing further than Dorothy's Oz. Somehow, her marriage seemed equally tenuous. Unshed tears collected in a knot high in her throat. "Why are you doing this? Don't you love me?"

He bent to peer into her eyes, and his mouth stretched into a smirk. "Why else would I marry you, Bea?"

She turned her face from him and sobbed until he retreated to the bedroom.

"Why? Indeed." She gasped as she slid down the wall to sit, arms hugging knees. Her stomach quavered, and her unease increased.

Before that night, he hadn't physically hit her, so she failed to define his controlling behavior as a kind of abuse. That night, though, beneath a moon shying behind thick clouds, he'd pulled her by the hair into the sea oats and slapped her until she whimpered, and he howled like a beast.

In the morning, she squatted over an absorbent stick to pee and found two pink lines. Tears blurred the sight as inner agony gripped her. She ran her palms over her taut stomach and thought, "How can I raise an independent-minded child with Roderick abusing me?" She wrapped the used pregnancy test in a sanitary napkin and toilet paper and pushed it to the bottom of the trash bin.

When he left to sing for the day, Bea rushed to gather her belongings and the little money she'd put aside. Her heart pounded as she stashed the bag. She'd leave that evening when Roderick fell asleep.

Her conundrum arose when she stopped by the bed as a farewell. The evening's brilliant starlight poured through their bedroom window and illuminated his peaceful features. Asleep in the room they had shared for less than a year, his hands folded like a child's in prayer, Roderick's beauty overwhelmed her.

Her resolve wavered. She recalled the thrill of their late-night telephone conversations that served as their dates. She'd believed he treasured her then, and she adored him. What changed?

Bea recalled the day of their hasty nuptials. After they exchanged vows, they dove to explore the corals, as was customary on the island. Swim thrice around the reef. Once for fertility, a second time for luck, and the final lap ensured lasting happiness.

He hadn't completed the last lap. He clutched shoulder to himself and winced. "Continue without me. Get us good luck." She swam, worried about her husband, hoping she'd gathered lasting happiness.

On the beach, they had wrapped each other in fluffy towels and drank in their good fortune and the golden sunshine. As she patted him down with the towel, though, he winced. she noticed a mark on the underside of his left arm, a raised, reddened circle about the size of her palm. He had slapped her hand away when she touched it.

"What's that?"

He hid the spot from her view. "It's from when I was a kid. Saltwater irritates it."

"You should have told me. Is that why you don't like to swim?"

He had flashed a mischievous grin. "Who said I don't like to swim?"

Bea pinched her lips at the remembrance and wondered about the mysterious mark he never adequately explained. She creeped to his side of the bed, pausing when his breathing slowed, careful of her own breathing and tip toed pace. With agonizing slowness, she pulled the sheet away from his arm until she could see the concentric circles, so like the bite left by a lamprey's mouth.

A pale ooze slicked its surface, wicked by his chest hair and the sheet. With trembling fingertips, she brushed the supposed wound. It left her fingers sticky.

Roderick rolled away with a grunt. His mouth fell open in a grunted snore.

Bea froze and held her breath, her eyes wide with apprehension. As his breathing resumed a relaxed pace, she, too, relaxed. Until she noticed the inside of his mouth.

During their marriage, Roderick disliked deep kisses, and from her vantage, Bea understood why.

Rows of needle-sharp, back-curving teeth ringed the upper and lower palate of Roderick's mouth, disguised on the bottom by his tongue. Their alien aspect rejuvenated Bea's resolve, and she rushed from their home, her retreat quick and quiet.

Lonely footprints in the sand marked her progress, footprints watered with her tears and the exuberant salt spray singing an accompaniment for her flight. She sniffed sadness with each step as she left her marital home, yet images of his psychological betrayals consorted with dawning nightmares within her psyche. Hits followed by tearful apologies, tender kisses, and compliments. Nothing pleased him.

Her tears obscured the starlight, casting halos around silvery centers. Circles, like his bizarre rings of teeth.

She shuttered, then ran. Each footfall kicked up a spray of sand and shell. They pounded her imprint upon the shore, and she shed abuses and humiliations with each reverberation. A foggy memory of childhood tales, of lamprey lycanthropy, wormed into her consciousness.

The mysterious waters hissed satisfaction. Insects called with the news, "Bea fled Roderick." It crescendoed, a great swell of sung celebration that ended in a resounding silence, where even the frogs ceased.

Bea stumbled in their silence and saw him framed by sea grasses and palm trees.

Roderick sniffed the air like a wild thing, and moonlight glinted off the teeth in his unhinged mouth. Several full circles of sharp, deadly pearls hungered for her blood.

She fled, her hair a midnight stream behind her slight figure. Her feet pounded the sand and ground the surf's rejects with her passage. She had no weapon and could not fight off his advances if he caught her, only her bag and whatever the sands provided.

With long lopes, he closed the distance, eager for the hunt. He'd devour her wishes for freedom, she knew, crunch her independence with greedy gulps. His tongue hung from his jaws, panting with pleasure.

She threw the bag at him. He dodged with ease.

With her progress across the beach, though, she revealed a galaxy of stars hidden in the sand, glints of solidified femininity left from millenna of women casting their cares to the powerful sea. With this sister silver, she could defend herself.

She scooped great handfuls of silvered sand.

He lunged.

She screamed and threw the sand into his face. As she hoped, he paused to brush it from his eyes with yelled curses. She ran. Stars spit in an arc, silver slivers lodged beneath his skin, multitudes leeching his vigor, bleeding his malice in garnet drips.

He burst forward, scrambling toward her.

She sidestepped and pulled a piece of driftwood to her aid. It burst into wooden shards over his head.

He roared, an inhuman howl.

Her breaths came in painful gulps as she rushed from him to the enigmatic lure of the sea. She crashed through the turbulent surf, leapt waves until the water deepened enough to welcome her. She dove.

He dropped to a knee on shore, pulled at his hair, and again howled. "You're my wife, Bea! You can't leave me!"

Phosphorescent plankton illuminated her progress, mini galaxies heralding her escape.

He prowled the shore, nostrils flared, lips pulled back from his dangerous teeth, but he lost her to the melodious waves. As the sun rose, he acknowledged her escape, at least for the moment. As he gasped salt-strewn air, he vowed to find her. To find her and punish her.

Bea allowed the waters to push her, exhausted, to a further beach. Her muscles betrayed her, and she stumbled like a newborn colt as she dragged herself through the sunrise-soaked sand. Tears mingled with the drying sea water on her face.

She'd shelter at her parents' until she could get her papers in order. She'd borrow money and take a flight to a new life, one with the hope of joy, but she knew better than to relax. She needed to protect her growing baby, needed to be wise, because each moon pregnant with ire could guide him to her. For protection until she reached a far-flung shore, she must bury herself within the silvered sand and pray for the protection of the dawn.

Bobbing Contest

Joel inhaled before plunging his head into the autumn water. He dove for an apple, pinned it against the barrel's edge. He'd win this game and impress Isabella, his true princess who dressed the part for the class Halloween party. The fruit spun and bobbed in the water, elusive. Behind his back, his wrists chaffed in their bonds.

Something in the barrel touched him, independent and mindful.

Not an apple.

Something moving of its own volition.

Long, lithe, a snake played its own game. It sunk fangs into Joel's chin, pulled him further into the barrel, held him until he stopped thrashing. He'd present the drowned body to his love, a beautiful cottonmouth with a taste for adolescent flesh.

Buback

Chill air rustled through the field, reviving Boo. She struggled against twine cutting into her wrists and wrested herself free of the post where the bullies had left her. As she fell to the ground, her overalls ripped. With a sigh, a golden haze fell like lint from the tear and disappeared into the nutrient-depleted earth. Boo scrambled to catch its threads, but they slipped through her fingers like youthful regret. She punched the earth where it disappeared and cursed. "Damn!"

As she examined the damage to the motley patchwork, a storm of anger flooded through her. She raised aching arms toward obscured stars, shaking a fist. She pulled her trembling hands through her straw-coarse hair, plotting.

"Fools tied me to a post instead of setting me on a throne as I deserve."

Clouds raced through the sky, revealing an amber moon sunk low on the horizon. A bonfire on the next hill sent sparks heaven-ward, giving her a beacon. She'd find people there, people who might know who did this to her, people crouching like Neanderthals as they shared roasted meats, mugs of warmed cider, and spine-tingling tales.

Her nostrils flared, and her stomach rumbled. She licked lips cracked from wind exposure and set off across the field of shorn maize. Dried husks crunched like autumn leaves as she made her way. She scooped up a discarded harvesting scythe. When rested upright, it stood taller than her, but its wood felt substantive as a decision in her hands.

She checked that her change purse remained in her pocket. Moonlight reflected off of the silvered metals of needles and sharp scissors. She fingered a spool of crimson thread in the bottom of the bag. Necessary items to repair her oft-patched garments. A cold breeze stole the word, "perfect" from her lips.

Something warm and furry brushed against her legs, and she startled for but a moment. A huge black tom cat bumped his head against her again, as though begging for attention.

Boo greeted the feline. "Oh, aren't you a beauty?"

He purred his approval. With tail held high, he scampered toward a fence, pausing to look over his shoulder and meow.

"Follow you? But my friend, I have a busy evening before me and must use the night well."

The cat yowled again, insistent.

Her laugh rustled the night breezes, causing the revelers atop the next hill to shiver. "Fine, for but a moment. I haven't time to waste."

Beneath a goat cart parked by the fence, a dozen cats, all black as pitch, huddled around a fallen nest. With noisy gulps, they feasted on two large crows. When Boo approached the birds, they reached their talons as though toward her away. They opened their pointed beaks in fear, but the gloss in their beady eyes dulled as the cats tore into their meat. The cats lapped up the blood and purred at their work.

The tom worked a figure eight through Boo's legs, pausing to swat at a stray bit of straw dragging from her hem. She stooped and scratched behind his ears. "You and your friends are a clever lot. I could use your help this evening. If you're willing."

Thirteen cats licked gore from their whiskers as she fashioned a loose harness about their chests and bellies. "You'll have more to eat this evening, I promise. I'll scare up some more crows for your pay." She grabbed the reaping scythe and stepped into the cart. The cats leapt over one another, eager for their promised feast.

The people at the bonfire atop the next hill laughed with the abandon only intoxicated people can manage. They clung to one another without regard for personal space, or perhaps because their own legs needed assistance holding them upright.

When Boo entered the glow from the fire, the group blinked with slow-dawning dread.

The praise leader pointed and screamed, "The devil's come!"

Her husband backed away into the cover of a stand of trees, abandoning his wife and the others as tactical war-remembrances flashed through his subconscious, PTSD controlling his reactions. Several people stumbled away from Boo and her strange conveyance team, but the farmer stepped forward, scratching his head. "Why, you're my scarecrow, aren't you?"

A smile stretched across her canvas face as she hoisted the scythe. "How nice of you to admit your guilt." She swung the blade into his flesh, relishing his look of slack-jawed incomprehension. "Should like to hang you on a post for a season. See how you like it."

Blood sizzled as it splashed into the fire. Boo licked a splattering that colored her cheek. She savored its metallic tang. Reaching into the farmer's chest, Boo cut his soul free and formed it into a patch. She slipped the patch into her front pocket and stepped over the farmer's corpse. "This will replace the one I lost. Let's see what else I can collect."

With another swing of the scythe, she freed the cats from their harness. They fell upon the farmer with gusto.

The farmer's wife threw a bottle at Boo, but it missed. Boo stepped forward like a ballplayer and cut the woman's soul free. The body slumped at her husband's feet, a look of shock frozen upon her features.

Two young men leapt at her, sons hoping to avenge their parents, but with ease, the blade passed through them. Their intestines bloomed from their severed abdomens, spilling into the stone ring meant to contain the fire. Flames singed them, browning the intestines like a string of fresh sausages.

The parish praise leader trembled under an unblessed wooden cross. "Get behind me, Satan."

Boo admired the tarnish that mottled the woman's soul. To comply with the request, Boo stepped to the side and sliced her open along her spine.

The rest of the bonfire company fled, but Boo had collected enough souls.

She licked chunks of flesh from her fingers, enjoying every mouthful as she considered placement of her new acquisitions. She flattened her newest patch and decided on irony. She chose the back of the overalls near the base of her spine. "Get behind me, praise leader with the tarnished soul," she chuckled. She threaded the needle, stripped off her garment, and sewed. When finished, she held the newly repaired overalls at arm's length to admire her handiwork.

"This will do nicely. Don't see how any farmer could resist asking me to guard their field when I'm such a well-dressed Buback."

She patted the cats fondly. "Thank you, my friends. We'll do this again next year. After all, every harvest some fool unwittingly sets me free."

One Wintery Halloween

One Halloween, the Martin family rushed to complete homework ("My teacher's such a jerk. Tonight's Halloween!"), eat dinner ("Eat your dinner, or no trick-or-treating."), and don costumes, Farrah a wicked witch and Charlie a faux-fur touting werewolf. They endured photos (Mo-om, we gotta go!) and instructions (Stick together. Look both ways before crossing the street. Stay in our neighborhood only.) before they raced to their mendicant night.

The kids trick-or-treated together, rushing from porch light to porch light like madcap moths. They aped their parent's insisted-upon phrase after each collected treat.

"Thank you."

Meanwhile, at home, the Martin parents handed out candy, full-sized Twix, with a cut crystal bowl of Reese's peanut butter cups set aside for themselves. Snug on the couch, they munched their sweet stash between doorbell rings. They enjoyed fewer intrusions as the night wore on, so they started a classic Universal monster movie.

Outside, the weather took an unexpected turn. Winds whipped not only autumn leaves but also snow squalls. White coated the kids, transforming midnight colors to wintery wonders. Neighbors' lights blinked off, denoting the end of the festivities in response to the deteriorated evening weather.

Stiff, shivering, demoralized, and red-cheeked, Farrah and Charlie returned home. They stomped inside and dropped their half-filled treat sacks on the floor.

Mr. Martin stopped them in the hall. "Excuse me, but you can't just walk in here."

The weary kids whined, "Why not?"

"Kids? Wow!" Mr. Martin laughed. "I didn't recognize you! The snow made you look like strangers!"

Benny the Beast

The hunger consumed him. He stalked the darkened street. Glowing eyes terrorized, gourds carved in grisly likenesses. One with fangs and narrowed eyes denied admission. He snarled. Candle flicker made it wink. How dare it! He kicked, grinding into the earthy mess, and growled.

He hurried past the pumpkin carnage and rushed the door. Others stood with sacks. He hunkered down and seized his prize. He ran from the throng, but one pursued.

"Benny, I know it's you!"

A burst of speed left her among the decaying leaves. He hid behind hay bales and tore into his prize. Chocolate, his favorite.

Apples

Macy raised the candy-coated apple to her lips. Its red matched her vibrant lipstick. She opened wide and bit. The candy cracked, and she pushed a bit of it into her mouth with her pinky finger.

Jan scowled. "Why you gotta be like that?"

Macy's brow creased. "Like what?" Her voice like spun sugar.

Jan opened her eyes wide at Tina, her lips pressed tight in "can you believe her?" exasperation.

Tina ducked her head over a secretive smile.

A bit of Macy's sweetness soured. "Like what?"

Jan spun to face Macy, elbows propped on wide knees, chin on her fists. "Like you're some kinda princess. Seriously, who're you impressing? It's just Tina and me here."

Macy's lower lip trembled, but her brows forecasted an angry storm. "I'm not trying to impress anyone. Just being tidy" Her rapid blinks and averted gaze prevented embarrassed tears from falling. She set her candy apple on a dessert plate, no longer hungry for it.

Jan shook her head, face tight with disgust.

Tina stood. "I've an idea." She walked into the kitchen where they'd made the candy apples earlier in the evening, before they'd handed out treats to costumed neighborhood kids. "My gram told me about an old Halloween tradition."

She grabbed a knife from the block and apples from a bowl on the kitchen table. She extended the knife and an apple toward Jan. "Peel the apple, hopefully in one long strip, throw it over your shoulder, and it's supposed to form the first letter of your intended's name."

"Really?" The airy sound returned to Macy. She licked her lips with anticipation.

Jan sighed. "That's kinda stupid."

Tina shrugged and put knife to fruit, spinning, spinning, until she produced a long, curling peel.

Macy watched on tiptoes to get a better vantage. Jan stole glances while pretending to consider her ragged manicure.

Tina tossed the peel over her shoulder. She and Macy leaned over it.

Macy traced the shape in the air above. "It looks like an L."

Tina nodded.

"No, it doesn't." Jan pushed Macy out of the way.

Macy squeezed between the girls. "In cursive. See? A loop, straight line, a smaller loop, and the bottom." She traced the shape again, smiling. She turned to Tina. "Whose name starts with L?"

Tina shrugged.

Macy chewed her lip. "Would the letter be a first or a last name?"

Tina laughed. "I guess it could be either."

"Lawrence, Labriolla, Littlejohn..."

Jan snorted. "That's it. Tina's gonna marry Benjamin Littlejohn."

Macy's eyebrows pinched together. "Why not? Tina, do you like him?"

She laughed and handed Macy an apple. "Your turn."

Macy rinsed the apple, closed her eyes, then, with bit-lipped concentration, carved the peel.

Tina watched. "In Norse mythology, the goddess Idunn's apples granted immortality."

Jan lowered her eyebrows and smirked. "You don't say?"

"I did it!" Macy hopped up, pleased. "One piece. Can you believe it?"

Tina nodded. "Now toss it over your shoulder."

Macy's grin widened. "I'm nervous!"

"About what?" Jan hoisted herself onto a high stool alongside the breakfast nook, far enough from the action to seem aloof, but close enough to see the results. "A stupid game?"

Macy's smile faltered. "Jan, please try to have fun."

"I'm having a blast watching you make an idiot of yourself."

Color rose in Macy's cheeks, but Tina placed a hand on her back and whispered, "Don't worry about her. Give it a toss. Let's see what happens."

"Ok." Her smile wobbled, widened. She closed her eyes, held the peel to her chin, then tossed it over her shoulder. It landed by her heels. She hunched over it and squinted. It had broken into two pieces. "D E." Her brow wrinkled. "Is that what you see?"

Tina's eyebrows shot high into her hairline. "Yeah. Maybe it stands for Ed Danvers?"

Macy widened her eyes. Her mouth formed a perfect O. "Ed Danvers? He's awesome! I've had a crush on him since grade school."

"First of all, I've had a crush on him since kindergarten. You copied because you always do. And second of all," Jan slid from the stool and pointed at the apple peels, "that looks like a P and maybe an O, so you're on crack. No way you're hooking up with Ed Danvers."

Macy pressed her lips into a thin line and crossed her arms. "It does so look like a D and an E. You're just jealous."

Jan spun, toe to toe with Macy. "Look here, toothpick, nobody thinks you're cute." Her nostrils flared as she looked up into Macy's shocked face. Her voice deepened to a near growl.

"Especially not Ed Danvers."

Tina grabbed another apple and tossed it into the air. "You know…" She caught it and tossed it again. "It's said if you carry apples and silver bells, you can walk through the many realms."

Macy and Jan turned astonished faces toward Tina.

Tina tossed and caught the apple. "Especially on days when the veil between the worlds thins."

Toss, catch. "Like Halloween."

Jan faced Tina. "What the heck're you talking about?"

Tina shrugged. Toss. Catch. "Apples. They're amazing."

"An apple a day keeps the doctor away, right?" Macy edged toward Tina.

"Something like that. So, Jan, it's your turn." Tina threw the apple to her. "Let's see your destiny." Tina waggled her eyebrows, grinned wide as a Jack-o'-lantern, and extended the knife, handle first, to Jan.

Jan took it and huffed. "Why not." She kicked Macy's apple peels toward the garbage bin.

"Hey!" groused Macy.

Jan peeled, biting deep into the flesh. The blade slid from the apple and bit deep into Jan's thumb.

"Damn it!"

She popped the injury into her mouth to catch the blood and tossed the apple and knife onto the island. She grabbed a first aid kit from a cabinet and ran her thumb under the faucet. She glared as tap water rinsed her wound. "Bet I need stitches."

"Let me see." Tina dabbed the thumb with a paper towel. She pressed to determine the depth of the cut. "I think it'll be alright." She sprayed antiseptic on the wound and bound it with a wide, highlighter-yellow bandage. "See? All better."

Jan tried unsuccessfully to bend her thumb. The bandage impeded movement.

"Might as well try your fortune, especially after you spilled your blood." Tina's eyes caught the light, giving her the glazed expression of a zealot. "Some would say that gives your foretelling extra reliability."

Macy handed Jan the apple peel. Her thin smile wavered an apology. "I brought all the parts."

Jan had produced an apple peel fat with apple flesh in one main piece and several small bits.

Blood had soaked into a small section.

"What the hell." She took the peel from Macy. "Here goes nothing." She tossed it over her shoulder.

They tilted their heads to consider the result.

"An A and a D," Macy interpreted.

Jan's lip curled. "I think that's an E and a D, actually." She straightened to her full 5 feet. "We all know what that means!" She threw back her shoulders. "And Tina said my forecast is stronger because I bled on the pieces." She wore a self-satisfied grin and blinked slow as a cat while she gloated. "Sorry, Macy."

Macy lifted her chin. "Don't be. I see an A, not an E."

"It's clearly an E." Jan adjusted the peel as she traced the shape with her finger.

"You moved it! You're not supposed to move it."

"Did not."

"Oh my gosh, you so totally did."

"I think I'd know if I moved the stupid peel. What's wrong, Macy? Don't think you can take the competition?"

"I don't have to worry about it, because you cheated!"

Tina slid the knife toward their heated discussion.

Jan slammed her hand onto the island, grabbing the knife. "Did not." Before she realized it was in her fist, she'd slashed. An angry red bloomed over Macy's cheek.

Macy pressed her hand to the cut and stepped away. Blood bloomed between her fingers.

Without thinking, Jan thrust into Macy's tiny waist. Macy doubled over, hands atop the new wound, eyes betrayed.

Jan drove the knife deep into Macy's warm ribcage. Blood and bile rooster-tailed.

Unsteady, Macy stumbled back, blood billowing, slicking the tile with abstract images. "Jan?"

Macy stumbled, eyes rolled, and she collapsed. Blood disgorged around her slight frame.

As though blinking free from a horrible dream, Jan dropped the knife.

Tina whispered into Jan's ear, "Better run, killer!"

Jan gabbered "Didn't mean to" and fled.

Tina sliced her apple in half, dipped it into Macy's pooling blood, and took a bite. Blood dribbled over her chin.

She raised her hands above her head, a tiny silver bell suspended from her fingers, and called in an ancient, breathy language, to her lover.

Her fallen apple peel glowed, widened, and formed an entry. Long, ebony-tipped fingers pushed through, pulled at the edges, ripped.

Lilith, raven-haired, leather-winged, Mother of Monsters, first wife in Eden, perfect in proportion and deadly beautiful, stepped through.

Tina moaned her name.

Offering

Connie left the offering as she did every year, and they partook. She hid behind insulated curtains to watch them devour and move on, picking bits from sharp teeth with long-nailed precision, to smile sweetly for the neighbors.

Neighbors and parents never realized without her, these darlings would revert to base instinct and demonhood. Her offering saved them again.

Connie closed the curtain until next Halloween.

Celebra-thing

We celebrate my birthday with spices and pumpkin, miniature candies and bobbing for apples. Friends caper in costumes. Squeals of surprise and terror reverberate through impromptu haunted houses, stealing the focus.

But, it's my birthday, and I want to celebrate me, not some towering, soul-searching god steeped in ancient lore. That's what they do, these fools who steal my day. They worship one whose name they can't properly pronounce.

Well, that will change tonight. I'm done allowing their disregard to overshadow my birthday. I'll conjure Samhain and feed him their souls. I translated and will proclaim the proper words.

Happy birthday to me.

Pumpkin Patch Prayers

Brittany's curls shook in the autumn breeze, a dark ocean of apprehension. "Kayla, this seems like a bad idea."

Kayla's jaw set with determination. "If you don't want to come, go back and hand out candy with Sabrina. I'm sure the trick-or-treaters will love seeing you." A steely strength played beneath her skin and within her narrowed eyes.

Brittany studied a swirl of browning leaves as they eddied at their side. "It's just so far from home, and nobody knows we're here."

Kayla lifted her cell phone. "We can call if there's trouble, right? But seriously, if you don't want to be here, scram. Uncle Linus said it had to be the most sincere pumpkin patch, and if you're going to ruin it with your squirrelly ways, well, you should leave now. I'll only have this opportunity once."

Aunt Sally had said this was all childish nonsense, though, and laughed as she recalled their visit to a patch years ago. Britt averted her gaze from Kayla's zeal. "I'm not going to ruin anything."

"Good, then let's go. We have to be there before the moon reaches its apex." Kayla's athletic legs picked up their pace. Brittany scrambled to keep up.

A group of elementary schoolers dressed as superheroes examined their sacks of candy as they walked by. "I got a Clark bar. Ever had one of them?" a caped crusader inquired of a shivering, dark-haired Amazonian warrior.

The girl shrugged. "Not sure."

Why are women's costumes often so skimpy, even for children?

Another knot of trick-or-treaters rushed up the walkway of a house festooned with spider webs and a giant, furry black spider that dropped to inches above their heads when they rang the doorbell. One of their number ran from the hairy monster, abandoning her glowing plastic collecting pail when she ran to her mother's comforting embrace.

Brittany smiled. *When we were little, that would've been me, running away, and Kayla would've retrieved my dropped candy for me.*

Kayla's profile appeared royal in the low light along the suburban streets, the kind of face cast onto ancient coins.

She's always been brave, despite everything she goes through. I don't know anyone who has such a hard life. Orphaned. Bullied at school and home. Overworked. Unappreciated.

Cries of "Trick-or-treat" became ghostly whispers the further the girls walked. Replacing the cheerful children's chorus were subtle scrambles beneath crunching leaves and warning hoots from the owl who watched the tiny movements of active rodents.

The girls held their breath when they passed the iron-gated cemetery, something they'd done since childhood to prevent ghosts from following them home.

Ghosts grow jealous of our breath and try to steal it. Britt shuddered. *Ghosts like most of Kayla's family, except the steps who mistreat and belittle her.* She quickened her pace.

They rounded the corner, climbed a hill, and reached Borland's Pumpkins at the top. The patch meandered around the centuries old house, scarecrows grinning from their sentry posts throughout. Kayla stuck to the shadows as she led the way to the heart of the vines. Mr. Borland was a nice man, but since they didn't ask permission to sit in his garden on Halloween night, it might be best to lay low.

They found an unharvested spot out of eyeshot, placed blankets on the chilled ground, and sat among gourds both massive and miniscule to wait. Kayla lit a small, cinnamon-scented candle which reflected in her troubled eyes.

"He'll be here soon. I know it." She hummed a haunting ditty as the flame sputtered.

Before long, her faith paid off.

Brittany clutched the neck of her sweater to her mouth to stifle a scream when, with a swirl of fog and a whoosh of wind that raised gooseflesh along their arms, a phantom rose pale in the moonlight. It startled a Southern Yellow Bat from its repose on a nearby woody rhododendron stalk. The little, winged rodent circled in frantic ellipses as though searching an escape.

Brittany pitched forward in a cowering crouch, but Kayla stood to greet her awaited salvation. Moonlight lent silvery streaks to her hair and refined her features until she glowed with beautiful anticipation.

"Welcome, Oh Great Spirit! We are honored by your presence. Thank you for coming." Her smile stretched wider and brighter than a Jack-o'-lantern's. She shivered with delight and wiped tears from her cheeks. She breathed, "I knew you would come! Please grant me my wish."

The spirit floated to Kayla on tumbles of fog. Thick tendrils of ghostly condensation circled Kayla as though pulling her into a waltz with the spirit.

Kayla gracefully complied.

Profound cold settled over Brittany, and she froze in place, squeaks of caution unable to escape her throat. Her strangled, "No," sounded like a moan, not a word, when the mists engulfed and obscured her cousin.

The harvest moon peeked through its veil of phantasmic clouds to pursue the fantastic scene, but its illumination came too late. Brittany covered her eyes and sobbed. The spirit had granted Kayla's wish for escape from the trials of this life. It had taken her to its realm.

Brittany sniffed. *What about my wish, though?* She blew out the tea light and watched its gray smoke ascend like a prayer. *I want my cousin back. Kayla's always been my best friend.*

The bat squeaked as it dove for its supper.

Brittany wiped her sleeve across her nose as though to brush aside selfishness. *Next year, I'll come here with sincere intentions.* She folded their blankets. Kayla's, threadbare and tattered, still smelled lemony like her. *I'll visit Kayla with the Halloween spirit. They'll return. I know they will.*

**This was written with the Peanuts' Halloween Special in mind, with Charlie receiving rocks for the holiday (Why? I don't know) and Linus searching for the perfect Pumpkin Patch. In my imagination, Brittany, Kayla, and Sabrina are relatives of the OG Charles Shultz gang. Can't you hear the magnificent Vince Guaraldi jazz haunting the girls' footfalls?

Belinda's Blue Halloween

Belinda watched the maple leaf float, flashing brilliant amber, to the ground. Heedless, her costumed schoolmates crunched it underfoot as they rushed to collect treats. The tang the crushed leaves released tickled her nose.

None of the classmates asked why Belinda didn't join the fun. They were used to Belinda sitting out, observing rather than participating. They didn't guess at or care about Belinda's longing for inclusion and yearning for friendship.

She complimented their costumes as they grabbed fistfuls from her treat bucket. Some smiled a thanks before they ran to collect more treats. None commented on her wizard robes or wand.

Her parents offered to accompany Belinda if she wanted to join the neighborhood fun, but she shrugged. "I'll hand out the candy." How could she explain? The night held too many potential traps for her jumpy personality, and to trick-or-treat with parents was for babies. And nobody in their right mind trick-or-treated alone.

The grandfather clock in her living room announced the end of trick-or-treats. She'd given away all of her candy in any case. Her parents would want her to get ready for bed anyway.

With a wistful sigh, Belinda wheeled her chair inside.

Pam's Perfect Costume

Pam drooped. She'd rejected costumes in the local places, even those in the "Spirited" popup stores, with their many options. None of the secondhand shops offered what she'd envisioned, either.

Her parents made it clear this would be Pam's last year for trick-or-treating, so the costume had to be perfect. She knew what she wanted. She dreamed of it every night since her parents' big disclosure about her aging out of her absolute favorite holiday's quintessential activity.

"Can't you just pick something already?" Her older brother Bob ran his hand through his wavy hair. "Seriously, we've been everywhere." He dropped his hand to his jeans with an annoyed 'smack.'

"Just one more place. Please?" She grinned up at him with what she hoped was a winning grin. "I'll buy you a pumpkin spiced latte with my own money as a thank you."

He scowled at her. "I'm not a girl." His attempt at anger cracked like a dropped tray of cinnamon rock candy. "Fine. One more stop." He wrapped her in a one-armed hug, mussing her hair. He leaned close. "But you'll have to get me an extra-large coffee."

She pushed him away, smiling. "Loaded with whipped cream!"

He parked in a lot in the little town of Fox Hollow. She fed coins into the meter as yellow leaves whispered with wind gusts and tangled in her hair. She snagged his hand and swung it as they made their way to the costume shop. He walked. She capered beside him like an enthusiastic puppy fighting a leash.

"Let's stop here." Pam tugged her brother to a shotgun Victorian boasting two huge glass display windows flanking the brass handled door. Manikins in the window paraded from one window to the other, the smallest child at the farthest left, with manikins advancing in size until at the far right, the tallest teen manikin extended a sack Santa would have been proud to claim. An adult manikin dressed as a witch leaned out of a painted doorway with a bowl brimming with popcorn balls and candy. Jack-o'-lanterns and fake leaves enhanced the tableaux.

A bell tinkled when they entered Carmine's Custom Tailoring. The place overflowed with fabric. Racks lined the walls. Stands jutted in a "v" pointing toward the back of the store and a long glass display counter where the elderly Carmine himself sewed what appeared to be a striped suit jacket, pins in his mouth. He nodded to them, raising a threaded needle like a salute.

Suspended from the high ceiling above circular tables dotted along the central corridor, special items like wedding gowns and afternoon tea dresses floated above their heads like bodiless specters. They swayed as Pam and Bob navigated toward a rack marked "teen."

Pam inhaled the scent of laundered clothes and a smoky herb, some sort of incense wafting from a painted bowl at the end of the counter. Hangers clinked as she waded into the costumes.

With a gasp, Pam spotted it, her ideal costume, the one she'd seen in her dreams. She leaped for a mask, a harlequin clown white as porcelain with rosebud lips. It rested on a dark wood table atop what could have been folded, silken pajamas, white and black, with puffball center accents and frilly ruffs at the neck, wrists, and ankles. She hugged it to herself. "This is it! I just wish it had a hat."

A thickly accented male voice rumbled, "Would you like to try it on, little lady?"

Pam jumped a little, startled, then giggled. "Yes, please."

"This way." He led her to a room of mirrors with wooden benches inside. "You said you wanted a pointy hat, no?"

She nodded. "Yes, please. A white and black one."

"White, with a black poof, no?"

Pam's mouth dropped open. "Yes. How'd you know?"

Carmine touched the side of his protuberant nose and smiled, displaying a scattering of yellowed teeth. He closed the door.

The costume fit perfectly. The mask, made of leather and painted a shiny white, tied in the back with a black ribbon that blended with her hair. She tipped her head to the side and struck a "ta da" pose. She'd need white gloves and sneakers. She could glue black puffs to the top of her old Tom's. Comfortable and exactly what she pictured. If only she had the hat.

"Young lady." Carmine knocked. "I found your hat. It'll be at the register when you're ready."

Bob's voice answered. "Don't get your hopes up. My sister's on some kind of mission, so don't be surprised if she's not happy with the costume."

The old man laughed. "Oh, she's satisfied. You'll see."

Bob's laughter joined Carmine's. "I hope so. There are only two days until Halloween!"

Pam slipped out of the clown get up, refolded it with care, and burst from the changing room. "You'll be happy to hear I may have found what I wanted."

Bob mimed clutching his chest, other arm whirling. "Say it isn't so!"

"I just need to see the hat."

Carmine sang out in his lilting voice. "Right here." He extended the perfect accessory.

"It's exactly what I need! I'm so happy!"

"You want gloves?"

She widened her eyes. "It's like you can read my mind!"

Carmine chuckled as he shuffled to one of the circular tables and picked out a pair for her. "These'll fit."

She tried them on to be certain, then bought the lot.

Wrapped in white tissue, the costume rested at the bottom of a handled paper bag which Pam swung as she escorted Bob to the coffee shop named MoonBeans.

Trick-or-treating couldn't come fast enough. Because she didn't want to ruin the surprise, Pam kept her costume under her bed, but she couldn't help trying on the mask and hat now and again. With the door shut and the blind drawn, she tied the ribbon behind her head. The image in the mirror perfectly matched her dreams, with its black curlicue falling into a tear at the edge of its left eye to the star-shaped beauty spot under the tiny, sculpted nose. Pam touched the smooth cheek and marveled.

Her mother called. "Dinner!"

An unfamiliar flash of anger swelled up in Pam. "Sure, I have to hop when she wants something, but when I need her help, it's at her convenience." With a sigh, she removed her mask, wrapped it in tissue paper, and replaced it in its bag under her bed.

While she cleaned the dishes after a taco dinner, Pam imagined her friend Georgie's face when she saw Pam's perfect costume. It helped that Georgie had confessed a fear of clowns ever since she'd watched 'It.'

"A character with my name gets killed by Pennywise! I don't like taking chances," she'd said. Pam bet Georgie'd scream when she saw Pam's disguise. She chuckled with wicked glee.

As she hung the last pot, Bob burst into the kitchen. "You're never going to guess what I found!" Before Pam could answer, he pulled a black kitten from inside his army jacket. It wiggled in his grasp and mewed, blinking wide, golden eyes.

"Oh my gosh!" She hopped with excitement. "Can I hold it?"

"Of course!" He nestled the soft ball of fur in her outstretched hands.

She rubbed her nose in its fluffy hair. It meowed, quiet but insistent. "Can I have it?"

"Let's find out." Bob cleared his throat when he'd entered the living room, standing straight as a soldier. "Mother. Father. Pamela and I would like to ask you for a huge favor."

Pam hopped from behind Bob and held out the kitten. "Look at him! Bob rescued him. I've named him Boo." She pulled the kitten back to nuzzle it again.

"You rescued it?"

Bob blushed, "Well, erm…"

"Bad people hurt black animals at Halloween time. You know that. So, Bob saved it."

Mom and Dad raised their eyebrows. Mom straightened, the way she did when about to say no. "Who's going to buy all of its supplies and food? What about its shots? This kitten might be sick."

Pam opened her mouth to protest, but Dad interrupted. "Your mother has a point. Plus, I don't remember saying you could have a pet."

Bob started to speak. "I'll pay for everything…" but Pam spoke louder, drowning out his calm and thoughtful words.

"So, you'll allow this helpless creature to be sacrificed, just because we didn't get permission to have a pet first?"

Mom bristled, but Dad rested a calming hand on hers, his voice an approaching storm as he looked at Pam.

"That's enough outta you, young lady."

"Mom, Dad, please. I will take care of all of the cat's expenses, even after I go to college, and Pammy will take care of cleaning the box and feeding it. Won't you, Pammy?" Bob only used her babyish nickname when trying to curry his parents' favor or when trying to annoy Pam.

She pressed her lips into a displeased line but shook her head. The kitten mewed with its tail pointed straight up.

Mom ran a finger along the kitten's back. Pam fought the urge to pull it away from her.

"It's a cute little thing." Mom raised her eyebrows at Dad, who closed the book he'd been reading. He removed his reading glasses and fixed his namesake with a penetrating stare. "And you'll pay for all of the supplies?"

Bob nodded. "Each and every one."

He shrugged and replaced his glasses. "It's up to your mother."

The kitten reached for Mom's finger, tiny needle-like claws extended. Pam secretly hoped Boo would scratch her.

"I guess so. But you clean up after it. And keep it off the furniture."

Bob smiled. He wrapped Mom in a hug, then shook Dad's hand. "Thank you. You won't regret this."

Pam didn't understand how Bob had such an easy way of interacting with their parents. Everything they said or did rubbed her the wrong way. Still, she now had a new kitten.

Dad buried his face in his book. Mom took her seat beside him and resumed knitting.

Bob nudged her. She frowned up at him, but he motioned to their parents. She shrugged.

He mouthed, "Thank you."

She rolled her eyes but breathed, "Thanks" before running upstairs with the kitten.

Bob followed.

Pam set Boo on her fuzzy purple carpet. "This is your room now." The kitten wobbled as it navigated the long strands of pile.

Bob crossed his arms and leaned his back on the doorframe. "I knew you'd like it."

She smiled up at him.

He shook his head. "Where'd you come up with that crazy rescue story, though?"

She shrugged. "Figured that'd make them want to keep him." She knocked the kitten over with a tiny shove. It splayed its claws. "Worked, didn't it?"

He snorted. "I'm going to the store to get a litter box and stuff. Want to come?"

"No, I think I want to show Boo my costume."

He chuckled. "Ok. See you in a bit."

"Close the door, please.

He did.

Pam smiled behind her mask at the kitten, getting close to its face. It backed away, fur puffed, back arched. Pam scooped it up and hugged it to her chest. "You're so cute I could just squeeze you to death!"

The kitten squirmed. It mewed. It scratched.

Pam realized the tightness of her grip. "I'm sorry." She set the kitten down, appalled by a continued urge to squeeze.

She sat beside the kitten, but it tumbled over itself and pounced on an errant elastic. She hid her mask when Bob returned to set up the food and litter box. When he clipped a tiny collar around Boo's neck, she bristled.

"Boo's my cat. I should put the collar on."

Bob laughed. "Then you buy its stuff." He ruffled the top of her head as if she were a little kid.

Her nostrils flared. She wasn't a little kid. Not anymore. In fact, she wouldn't be allowed to trick-or-treat ever again after this year. So unfair.

No sooner had Bob left than she scrambled for her mask. Somehow, she felt more herself in it. Safe behind its porcelain-like perfection, she prepared her pillowcase.

On Halloween night, she dressed with care. The full-length mirror proclaimed her outfit perfect until Boo leaped on the ruffle on her left ankle and snagged the material. The kitten cried, its nail stuck.

Pam screamed, "No!" Breathing heavily, she picked up the delicate, meowing miscreant. "You've ruined it!" She squeezed the tiny belly. Boo mewed and wiggled, but when he hissed, Pam came to herself. She shook her head to dislodge her anger. Nobody would notice a tiny snag, but she'd been angry enough to kill. She set the kitten on a pillow designated as its bed and left to meet Georgie.

Georgie, dressed as a superhero, actually backpedaled when she saw Pam. "Oh my gosh! You scared the life out of me."

Pam laughed. "You're still breathing. Let's go."

Her parents delayed their departure. "Just a few photos. You girls look so cute!"

Pam bristled. "Cute?" She tapped her foot, her annoyance growing with each passing second. "Come on. Curfew's at 8!"

"Be safe, you two." Her parents called. "Don't eat any of the candy until we check it."

"Like they would know what to look for anyway," Pam grumbled. Outside, underway for candy collecting, she turned a quick cartwheel and admired the way her costume seemed to glow in the dusk.

"You really look creepy, you know."

Pam shrugged. "So."

"You should've warned me."

The mask hid Pam's curled lip. She ran ahead to claim more fun sized chocolates in her pillowcase.

"Wait up." Georgie jogged, huffing to breathe.

"Do you have your inhaler?"

"No, so slow down, will ya?"

Pam smirked. No, she wouldn't.

She left Georgie as she rushed ahead. She'd raced down two cul-de-sacs and up a hill when she heard a familiar voice. The school bullies harassed a group of three younger kids.

Pam's blood boiled. Her costume lent anonymity, and from therein, she wrested courage. She marched up to the confused group. She deepened her voice and interposed herself between the bullies and the bullied. "Leave them alone."

"What have we here? A clown?" The lead bully, Ish, sneered.

The littler kids darted for the next house without even a thank you. *Ingrates*, Pam thought.

Ish tried to push Pam, but she sidestepped, bouncing like a boxer. A strange exhilaration refreshed her, lending a looseness to her movements, a sharpness to her vision. She swung her bag of candy, connecting with Ish's friend's head. A pillowcase filled with candy wouldn't harm anyone, but one filled with candy and the rocks she'd plunked into the bottom for just such an opportunity did the trick. Blood bloomed from the corner of his eye. A second swing caught Ish square in the face. His nose burst.

Pam laughed, pleased with the festive new splotches of color on her pillowcase. She took another swing, but Ish and his friend backed away.

"What the hell, man?"

"That's not okay!"

"I think you broke my nose!"

She rushed to swing again, but an arm encircled her waist.

"That's enough."

She spun to find a grim-faced Bob.

"Your friend came back alone, so I came to find you."

He spit after the retreating bullies. "Let's get home."

"No." Pam crossed her arms. "I'm not done trick-or-treating."

"Pammy, baby," he stooped to look her in the eyeholes of her mask. "It's done. Look around. The house lights are off. There are no more trick-or-treaters."

"I'm not done." Pam marched up to an unlit house and rang the doorbell. When nobody answered, she kicked their Jack-o'-lantern.

"Seriously, kid, what's wrong with you?" Bob grabbed her hand and pulled her toward home.

Pam growled, deep in her throat, pent up anger brimming. "I'm not a kid. I'm not a baby. And I'm not done trick-or-treating."

He stopped and stared open mouthed at her. "Do you hear yourself?" He shook his head.

"Do you hear yourself? I was a hero back there, and nobody even said thank you! I protected those little kids."

"What little kids?"

"The ones Ish and his sidekick picked on."

He paused to stare again, brows knitted over concerned eyes. "There were no other kids, Pam. Just you and those boys."

She glared behind her impassive mask. She couldn't believe her brother sided with those jerks.

"Let's just get home."

Home, Pam thought, where her parents would 'check her candy.' They always ate their favorites during the check. They thought she didn't know, but she did. Mom loved Kit Kat Bars. Dad's favorite was Clark. She'd added some to her sack along with the rocks, candy soaked in chemicals especially for them.

She handed Bob her pillowcase and turned a cartwheel. She loved her costume, and the best part of it was because she was basically done growing, she could wear it again next year.

She smiled behind her perfect mask.

Mrs. Kernel the Witch

All the trick-or-treaters knew not to visit Mrs. Kernel's. Their whispers carried on autumn breezes as they cast distrustful glances at her shabby house.

"She's a witch."

The fallen leaves crunched beneath their feet as they hurried past.

"Witches eat children."

Bats squeaked overhead as they crossed the street to avoid her abode.

"She gives poisoned treats."

Inside the run-down cottage, lonely Mrs. Kernel sat knitting by the door, her rocking chair's creak louder than the crack and pop of the fire in her hearth. She spent her month's income on candy, hoping for a visitor on Halloween.

None came

Betty Bumblebee and Bogies

The kids clamored for the closest position, shoving masks askew and pushing treat bags toward doors. Their high-pitched voices demanded "Trick-or-treat!" of neighbors who dumped chocolate bar ransoms to restore quiet to the autumn evening.

Bruce trudged through fallen leaves after the crowd of little ones, pursuing a preschooler in a Betty Bumblebee tutu. She circled back, her twin pony tales bobbing as she bounced, to extend her bag.

"Heavy, Daddy. You carry, please?" He dumped the goodies into a pillowcase he carried and returned her empty bag. "Thank you!" She ran to catch up with the pack of kids.

He unwrapped a fun-sized bite of chocolate and popped it in his mouth, savoring the creamy sweetness melting over his tongue. *Glad this is a safe neighborhood. No razorblades or pins to worry about from this crowd.* He leaned against a lamppost and chewed the nougat center of the candy. *Don't know why the Mrs. Insisted I walk with our girl. The other parents trust. Not my wife, though, so here I am.*

A soft voice sent gooseflesh over his arms. "Sure is nice seeing a father taking an interest in his children."

If the face is half as sexy as the voice... Moon-pale skin, crimson lips, and slanted dark eyes greeted his gaze. Her tight little body brushed against him as she followed the pack of children.

His jeans tightened in reaction. He cleared his throat. "Child. I've only got one." He fell in step beside her, fascinated with her swaying hips. Two little ones he hadn't notice skipped from her shadow and joined the pack of squealing children. He pointed to them. "Yours?"

Her laughter sounded metallic, like wind chimes. "My helpful little Bogles."

The thin, fairy-winged little ones wrapped arms with Bruce's bumblebee as though preparing to skip down the yellow brick road on an adventure through Oz. Bumblebee started and giggled before skipping with them.

He hefted the pillowcase of sweet loot over his shoulder. His walking companion carried no bag. Better yet, she wore no rings. *A single mom?* He used his thumb to twirl his wedding band, resenting its presence. "Do our kids go to preschool together?"

"Don't think so. We're not from these parts." He detected an accent. Something Irish, maybe? *Fiery Irish.*

The pack of kids yelled, "Thank you!" before rushing up a new walkway to ring another doorbell.

"Oh? Where're you from?"

"The Summerlands. Ever heard of them?" A streetlight set her hair aglow like a dark halo while casting her face in shadow.

"Don't think so. What brings you to these parts?"

Her accent thickened. "Samhain. We love collecting."

"Trick-or-treating fans, huh? Why'd you come here, though? Our little plan's rather low key, I understand."

She strode ahead. "We like the pickings." She paused to smile up at the star-filled sky. White teeth glinted in the moonlight. "'Twas nice ta be a-meetin' ye."

"Wait, are you leaving? I don't even know your name."

She turned without another word and disappeared into the shadows.

Bruce stepped into the gloom. *Where'd she go?* He shook his head, feeling a bit drunk, though he'd not imbibed. *Hot little thing. Probably best she's gone. I might've been tempted to do something my marriage might regret.*

The trick-or-treaters had continued their pursuit, and they neared the end of the block. He hurried to catch up with the knot of kids, calling his Betty Bumblebee, but no Betty answered his call. He stepped among the trick-or-treaters, searching. "Say, do you know where my little girl's gotten to?"

A wide-eyed superhero shook his head while a bonneted Bo Peek shrugged. "Sorry, Mr. What's she dressed like?"

He swallowed a gulp of disbelief. "Betty Bumblebee. She's about this tall." He held out his hand about waist high.

An elementary-aged bride scratched beneath her veil. "I remember her. Haven't seen her in a bit, though."

Cold sent chills down his spine. His volume increased with mounting panic. "What do you mean? She's with two fairies."

All the kids shuffled around, shaking their heads. Betty Bumblebee was not with them. "Don't remember fairies, just the Bumblebee." "Saw her last at that house." An astronaut pointed to where Bruce collected his girl's candy.

He dropped the sack of candy and raced back the way they came, screaming for her until he grew hoarse. "Please," he begged the night air, but the stars blinked, unresponsive in the Halloween sky.

Nema

Nema donned an angel costume for Halloween. A scented breeze swirled crisp, browned leaves. She sought trick-or-treaters, since she had no friends, no longer knew anyone. Those she knew died long ago. She blended in with a group of five strangers about her age, haunting their steps.

"Boy, it's cold!" one wrapped his vampire cape tighter about his shoulders. At a decorated house, an ancient woman hunched over her cane. She clucked her tongue at the group, all toothless grin, until she recognized the ghost among the living.

She cackled, pointing. "I'll join you next year! We'll trick-or-treat together, Nema!"

Crossroads Inn on All Hallow's Eve

Chyna applied the last of her spooky glamor makeup with a flourish of purple glitter. She tested the glue holding her fangs in place with a tap of her tongue. They held, secure as her own naturally grown canines. A little fluff of her cleavage in a black dress cut deep enough to satisfy Elvira, strappy black heels in place, and she nodded to her friend Sharon.

"'Bout time." She slid the sleeve back on her flesh-colored leotard to consult the time on her fitness tracker. "If I'd have known you were going to take so long…"

Chyna slipped her arm around Sharon's thin waist in a half hug. "Come on. We don't want to be late!" She scooped a cape from the arm of their couch. "You make a cute belly dancer, by the way." She fluffed the brightly colored layers of skirting that fell like flower petals around Sharon's lean legs. The movement caused the hip belt of tiny brass bells to tinkle and chime.

"Thanks for lending me the costume." Sharon donned an 'Old Nor'Eastern' hoodie. "Can't believe you just have this stuff laying around."

Chyna pushed her friend's thick, dark hair back from her face. "No problem. You know me. I love dressing up." She frowned. "I wish you'd let me do your makeup, though."

"Uh-uh." Sharon backed away, hands warding her off. "I'm girlie enough in this get up as it is."

Worry wrinkled the space between her brows. "Are you sure they'll even let us in the door?"

"I'm positive." Chyna grinned at her friend, showing her fangs. "You worry too much. The IDs look great, and they might not even ask for them."

Sharon sighed. "Fine. We'd better get going or we'll miss the bus." She locked their dorm room behind them.

They made their way through pockets of reveling classmates in the hallway. One very drunk man jumped in front of them with a loud, "Boo!" They sidestepped him with frowns.

Their neighbor, Jo, called them. "You guys aren't really going to the Crossroads, are you?"

Chyna leaned close to her and whispered, "We are."

Jo crossed her arms over her ample chest, a disapproving moue pulling her lips. "I heard it's not safe," she lowered her voice to a barely perceptible whisper, "and if the RA or Dean find out, you could get into trouble."

Chyna slid her arm around the bigger girl. "That's why nobody should say anything about what we're doing. So, we won't get into trouble. Right?" She smiled up at Jo and patted her lower back. "Happy Halloween!"

"Just be careful, okay?" Jo's brows clustered like a threatening storm. She grew louder. "Okay?"

"We will, Mom!" Chyna blew a kiss to Jo, grabbed Sharon's hand, and hurried to the end of the hall.

Since the line for the elevator stretched all the way to the lounge, they opted for the stairwell. It echoed with the refrain from "Monster Mash" and reeked of stale alcohol.

When they pushed through the fire door, they inhaled crisp October air. Leaves crunched underfoot as they hurried to the bus stop.

Even the bus driver, face partially obscured by a white Phantom of the Opera Broadway half mask, wished them a happy Halloween as they claimed seats up front. She'd hung rubber bats from the ceiling along the aisle. "The Purple People Eater," "Werewolves of London," and "Thriller" played through the bus's speakers before they reached their stop.

"Thanks, Aggie!" Chyna and Sharon called as they skipped down the stairs.

"You girls be careful tonight, y'hear!"

Chyna spun to face the bus driver. "You mean there might be weirdos out?"

"Exactly."

"But Aggie," the girls grasped each other's hands, conspiratorially close. With huge smiles, they said in unison, "We ARE the weirdos!" They fell into fits of giggles as the bus pulled away.

"I've always wanted to say that!" Sharon stretched her arms toward the star-dazzled night sky with its silvery clouds obscuring a full moon.

"Me, too! Remember watching 'The Craft' when we were, like, twelve?" Chyna picked up a purple petal from Sharon's skirting. "I bind you, Sharon," she skipped around her friend, wrapping her with the bit of fabric, "from harming others or yourself."

"Oh, you!"

Their voices echoed along the deserted street.

They raced along the sidewalk outside of closed storefronts and quaint shops, their windows all decorated with fake autumn leaves and colorful gourds. As the girls rounded the bend leading out of town, jazz music drifted on smoky breezes from the hollow and the Crossroads Inn.

Sharon paused, fingers resting on her throat as though concern lodged there.

Chyna grabbed her hand and tugged. "Come on! We're almost there!"

Sharon's hesitance melted with Chyna's enthusiasm as they rushed down the hill.

The Crossroads Inn rose from the west side facing the town of Minster. A huge, log-hewn building that predated much of the historic area, it seemed to steep the area with its intrigue. Some said The Crossroads welcomed guests before any settlers came from overseas, even before the native folk who called the area of northeastern Pennsylvania home. Many musical greats got their start by performing at the Crossroads in this little nothing of a town.

Celebrities visited, too, and sports stars. Even politicians stopped to whet their whistle. Somehow, the Crossroads attracted high-caliber clientele despite its unfortunate location smack dab in the middle of farm country and at least an hour's drive from any city of importance.

The girls used the white-painted crosswalks to reach their goal.

"I can't believe we're here!" Chyna's voice quivered with excitement. She squeezed Sharon's hands. "Thanks for coming with me."

Sharon's gaze darted like a nervous filly's, but she smiled at her friend. "Wouldn't miss it for the world."

Chyna reached up on tippy toes and kissed Sharon's cheek. "You really are the best!"

Sharon rubbed the resultant black cherry lipstick mark with the edge of her hoodie sleeve as they pushed open the heavy, carved wooden door.

Once they stepped inside, smoke and music hit them like a tangible wave. A live jazz band, dressed as Mexican sugar skulls in black tuxedos, wailed. Laughter and chatter punctuated as an undercurrent. Though almost every place in Pennsylvania boasted a smoke-free environment, cigarette, cigar, and pipe smoke mingled with the skunkier bongs, creating a haze at Sharon's eye level.

A bouncer large as a Pittsburgh Steeler's linebacker blocked their admittance with one muscled arm. "ID?" His voice rumbled with authority.

The girls made eye contact with one another, growing a bit pale in the low lighting, before pawing through their tiny wristlets and producing their falsified bits of plastic.

The bouncer barely glanced at the cards, staring hard enough at the girls to bore holes directly into their subconsciouses. "Happy Halloween." He handed the plastic back without breaking eye contact.

"You, too!" Chyna waggled her black nailed fingers at him as she led Sharon into the crush of partying people.

Although everyone wore costumes, Chyna recognized many prominent people. The town's mayor sipped a brilliant red cocktail with a local state representative who nursed a black salt rimmed, glowing orange margarita. Professors danced with costumed students, some sophomores like Chyna and Sharon. Shop owners sat around high tables, their feet resting on silvery rings of elevated stools. Three men dressed Amish, but Chyna didn't believe their clothes to be costumes. The homespun of the fabric felt too authentic.

A high-heeled woman sidled up to them. Dressed in a navy-blue skirt that barely covered her rear assets, spiderweb tights, a revealing, sleeveless tuxedo top, and a bellhop-type cap atop her cropped hair, she could have stepped out of a 1940's film. An old-fashioned wooden tray hung from a pale blue cord around her neck. It displayed books of matches marked "Lucifers," three silver Zippo-style lighters, a row of skinny cigars, and a long, white feather.

"You gals look great!" Her voice sounded artificially high pitched and breathy. "Are you entering the costume contest?"

"Sure are!" Chyna smiled. "Where do we sign up?"

"Right over there." The cigarette girl motioned with her chin. "Good luck!"

"Thanks!" Chyna grabbed ahold of Sharon's hand, and they pushed through to the indicated table.

"We'd like to sign up for the costume contest, please."

A heavy-lidded beauty in her beaded flapper dress handed them pens. "Fill this out. They'll make an announcement when the contest begins. You'll line up at the foot of the stage stairs and walk across when your name's called." She raised her pencil-thin eyebrows.

"That's some commitment to authenticity," admired Chyna. "Just like the ladies from the Roaring Twenties."

"You'll be told where to stand after that." The flapper pursed her rosebud lips. "Got it?"

"Sure do!" Chyna filled out her form before handing the pen to Sharon. The red ink surprised her for a second.

Sharon leaned over and whispered in Chyna's ear, "I've got to go to the restroom."

Chyna strained to search.

Sharon tapped her shoulder. "It's there," she mouthed. "I'll be right back."

Chyna leaned into Sharon and motioned for her to bend to hear. "I'll get us some drinks, K?"

Sharon smiled and shrugged. She disappeared in the direction of the restroom still shaking her head.

Chyna sidled up to the edge of the bar. Fog bubbled up from behind it, sending atmospheric tendrils reaching for the mirror-backed shelves of alcohol. A young brunette in his twenties dressed in an old-fashioned racing uniform, complete with goggles, leather hat, and handlebar mustache, leaned over the gleaming mahogany bar. "What's your poison, little lady?"

His intense stare brought a blush to her cheeks. She giggled. "Um, what do you suggest?"

He tipped his head back into a knowing nod, a half-smile turning his mustache up at the ends. "I'll fix you up."

"Two, please." She cleared her throat when he turned back, eyebrows raised. Her cheeks' heat intensified. "My friend went to the restroom."

He smiled, his perfect teeth glinting white in the low light. "Your boyfriend?"

Her face would combust in a moment if he continued to look at her that way. "No. I don't have a boyfriend. My girlfriend. She's in the - well, you know."

He slid two stemmed glasses to her. "This one's a Spooky Sangria." He pointed to the goblet with the red concoction. "Apples, blood oranges, and cherries." A plastic skeleton peeked over the rim. "I think you'll like it." Another smile. "And this one's a Caramel Apple." Caramel dripped over the lip of the apple-adorned glass. He leaned closer. "For your friend."

Chyna licked her lips. "They both sound amazing. Thanks." (She wondered why she sounded so breathy.) She cleared her throat. "How much do I owe you?"

His half smile raised the left side of his mouth. He exaggerated looking around before he whispered, "No charge." He lifted his eyebrows and straightened to his full height. "Happy Halloween." The fog machine behind the bar kicked into high gear. He disappeared into the resultant cloud.

"Thanks. Happy Halloween!"

She sipped the sangria. It burned with sweetness. She closed her eyes as it warmed her throat. "Mmmm."

A sultry alto voice breathed near her ear. "Looks tasty."

Chyna's eyes flew open.

An Elsa Lancaster-style Bride of Frankenstein, complete with black and white makeup, stared into Chyna's drinks. She touched her black-painted nail to the caramel rim of Sharon's drink. She tipped her head back and allowed the caramel to drip into her mouth. Startlingly, even the interior of her mouth, including the tongue, lacked color.

"Must be the lighting," Chyna thought. *"But what's Sharon going to think about this lady fingering her drink?"*

As if summoned by Chyna's thoughts, a wide-eyed and pale Sharon joined the odd pair. "You're not going to believe what I just saw." Her hands shook. "These women were riding on enormous black goats." She pointed. "There was a parade of them over there."

The pale, black-nailed finger of the bride dipped into the caramel of Sharon's glass again. Chyna pulled it away, glaring, imposing her shoulder between the drink and the strange woman.

"Calm down," Chyna said. "I'm sure it's some Halloween hijinks. This place is full of fun."

Sharon shuddered, her wide gaze darting about the room. She mumbled, "Not sure about the fun part."

"Oh, don't be silly." Chyna edged Sharon away from the insistent, interloping fingers. "Here, have a drink. It's called a caramel apple."

Sharon took the drink without looking at it. She whispered, "Something's off here. Can't you feel it?"

A fair-haired maiden wrapped in the sheer, white linen of an ancient Greek drifted to them, a bemused smile on her face. She pointed to the drink in Sharon's hand and, with a wistful smile, shook her head. "I wouldn't drink that, dear. Sometimes all it takes to trap you is one pomegranate seed."

Sharon looked from the drink to the woman, confusion wrinkling her forehead. "What?"

The forgotten bride swooped in like an albatross. "I'll take it if you don't want it, dear." Her small mouth opened to reveal tiny white teeth like seed pearls stitched to black satin.

Sharon surrendered the drink. "Sure."

"Hey, give that back!" Chyna's head swiveled from the bride to her friend. "That's Sharon's drink."

The bride licked the rim with her blackened tongue, irisless eyes unblinking.

Sharon shivered. "It's ok. I don't want it, anyway."

"But I got it for you."

"Really, it's ok. I'll pay you back." Her hands trembled as she extracted a twenty from her wristlet.

"No, keep it." Chyna whispered, "The drinks were on the house. Can you believe it?"

Sharon glanced at Chyna's half-consumed glass, then into her eyes. "On the house?"

Chyna's shy smile crept across her face. "Yeah."

A man in black leather hot pants and a studded vest offered hors d'oeuvres from a silver tray. Both girls refused politely. Three small people covered in ghostly sheets leaped toward the tray, but the waiter raised the hors d'oeuvres above his head and continued through the crowd.

Chyna felt a gaze and turned toward the bar. The waiter smiled, his attention unwavering. Chyna blushed in response. She said to Sharon, "I'll get you another drink."

"I don't want one."

Chyna ignored her friend and danced to the man with the handlebar mustache. She almost collided with another small ghost, but with the exception of a shove to her thigh, the ghost avoided the impact.

"Hey." Chyna glared after the small figure as it disappeared into the crush of people.

She pulled herself onto a raised brass bar stool and asked the mustached bartender, "What's with all the kids here?"

He chuckled. "Kids?"

"Yeah, the pack of trick-or-treaters dressed as ghosts. One almost pushed me over."

He scanned the room. "I don't see any kids."

"They were just here. About four or five of them."

He shook his head.

Sharon tugged at her elbow. "Chyna, let's go. Please."

"Why? The costume contest hasn't even started." She smoothed her long, black gown. "I worked hard on these." She blinked at Sharon. "Oh my gosh. You have to take off that hoodie. Nobody can see your outfit." She set her drink on the bar and manhandled Sharon out of her hoodie. "Great. Now your hair's a mess. Where'd you find the lady's room?"

She hopped off of the bar stool, retrieved her drink, and guided Sharon through the crowd to the restroom. Tapestries hung in the hallway leading to the ladies' room, stitched silver and gold depicting tarot card art. Chyna recognized the hanged man, the tower, the moon, and of course the devil. The bar noise muffled inside of the restroom.

A woman whose junkie costume might not have been a costume offered a sample cup. "I'll pay you for your pee."

"Um, no thank you."

Chyna turned her attention to Sharon. The girls locked their wide-eyed gazes and pressed their lips tight against all they wanted to say to one another. The junkie's reflection twitched in the mirror, holding the sample cup like a life raft. A giggle broke free from Chyna's reserve. To cover, she pulled Sharon's arms to induce Sharon to squat so she could fuss with her hair. "As soon as the costume contest is over, we'll leave, ok?"

Sharon nodded with enthusiasm.

In the cool hallway, tapestries of the tarot cards featuring swords and the death card led them to red carpeting and circular tables inhabited by masked patrons. The metal music played by the live band seemed out of sequence, somehow, and when the assembled group turned to gawk not at the thrashing mosh pit or the hair band but at the girls, Sharon pulled Chyna back into the hallway.

"This is the wrong room," she whispered as she retreated from the watching eyes. They bumped into something solid.

They'd collided with a floor-to-ceiling bird cage. Inside, two bald headed birds squawked, flapping their dusky feathered wings. "Vultures," Sharon breathed as the avians hopped on their bare branches to loom over them.

Across from the aviary, a stone archway led to a set of marble stairs. Chanting echoed from its depths.

Both girls' eyes widened.

"We have to go see!" Chyna's blood pumped excitement through her small frame as she slipped from Sharon's grasp and rushed down the sweeping stairway. The bottom spilled into a vast, circular room with archways leading to further destinations. A group of hunched-over figures costumed in dark woolen hooded robes breezed by the girls as they hurried to an offshoot, leaving the scent of cinnamon and cloves in their wake.

Chanting swirled with metal music and jazz, creating an eerie, echoing cacophony.

Sharon spun her friend to face her. "Are you crazy? We have no business being down here!"

From one of the arches, a misshapen ball skittered to a rest a few paces from Chyna's foot. A diminutive woman in a revealing gray and white bunny costume rushed after it, giggling. Her oversized cotton tail brushed Chyna's hand when she bent to retrieve what was not a ball but a human skull.

Sharon gasped.

The bunny wobbled on her high heels before rushing back the way she'd come.

"Let's just take a peek." Chyna sidled up to the nearest stone archway and leaned inside. Torches sputtered, casting flickering light over walls of bones, a swept dirt floor beneath and a domed ceiling above. The musty stillness of the place was interrupted by a small group in Victorian mourning clothes kneeling before a metal placard. They took turns as they slammed their heads to its base. Blood dripped to the dirt which sucked it in greedily with audible slurp. The eldest veiled woman, next in the mourning party's progression, cracked her skull, setting her hat askew while a sheet of blood poured over her anguished features. The group moaned in unison and continued to hammer the plaque with their foreheads.

Sharon shook as she pulled Chyna to the stairwell. "We need to go. Now."

Chyna followed her up the stairs. "How peculiar." Her voice floated, dreamlike, and her movements wavered and swayed. "Did you see them hitting their heads?" She wavered, drunken. "But those costumes looked authentic."

Sharon slipped an arm around Chyna's middle to support her as they ascended. She grumbled to the still muttering Chyna, "What was in that drink?"

A group of what looked like 13 Girl Scouts trooped by. Instead of wearing tan or green, these young ladies, none of whom looked any older than 16, wore red uniforms, complete with badged sashes or vests and jaunty barrets. Their gazes appraised Chyna, who had sunken into Sharon's assistance, and they whispered behind their hands.

Their sneers and covert, backward scrutiny annoyed Sharon. She wiped sweat from her brow and called, "I thought scouts were supposed to be helpful?"

Their giggles answered as they clumped together to hurry up the stairs.

At the top of the stairs, Sharon leaned against the carved knoll post to catch her breath and assess. "Which way to the exit?"

The vultures loomed from their cage. Sharon recognized the velvety flocked wallpaper along a hallway and resumed her support of her friend. "Chyna, you have to walk. I can't carry you."

Chyna brought her hand to Sharon's cheek and listed close enough to waft alcohol breath. "You're so nice to me, even after everything I've done to you."

A door with an art nouveau nude stained-glass panel opened. A man who could convincingly portray Lurch from the Addams family emerged with a dome-lidded silver platter in his gloved hand. He moaned deep in his throat as he waited for the girls to pass.

Sharon stilled for a moment. "Oh? What have you done to me?" Her heart plunged and her stomach roiled. Why had she asked? "Never mind. It's just the alcohol talking. Let's get home."

"Can't leave yet." Chyna's words slurred a bit, and her eyes had trouble with focus. "Costume contest."

"Damn the contest. Let's go home."

"Interesting word choice." A woman in a sparkling Jessica Rabbit dress which displayed her ample curves to great advantage snaked her arm through Sharon's. Heady, exotic perfume engulfed her as the woman's sashaying hip bumped Sharon's with each stride. "The contest is about to begin."

Sharon tried to extricate herself, but the woman's grip constricted. "Sorry, but we have a bus to catch." Sharon couldn't escape the woman's grip.

"Your friend signed up for the contest. She signed." The woman flashed a movie star worthy grin. "You can go, if you want, though, since you didn't sign." The woman pointed her bloody red fingernail. "There's the exit." She pushed Sharon.

The crowd swelled around her, and she lost sight of Chyna and the red-dressed woman. She stood on tiptoes, but couldn't find them.

"What's the matter, darling?" An attractive man Sharon thought she might recognize touched her arm. His dark eyes brimmed with concern. The way his black curls framed his face gave him the look of a work of art rather than flesh and blood.

Sharon pulled her arm from his over-hot grip and rubbed where he'd touched. "I can't find my friend."

"Samhain crowds are always terrible. Everyone comes, what with the veil so thin."

Sharon blinked at him. "I'm sorry?"

The man smiled, straight white teeth behind kissable lips. He exuded charisma. "Never mind."

Something seemed so familiar about him. "Are you an actor or something?"

His smile crinkled the corner of his eyes. "Yes, I am. You'll be seeing me on the silver screen soon." His thick lashes cloaked his luminous eyes. "I also sing. I've a single coming out tonight. Hope you'll like it."

Sharon blushed. "I'm sure I will."

"Me, too." He nodded, knowing.

The band and the crowd quieted. A tall, thin, androgenous person clothed in Las Vegas feathers strode the stage as the band pulled their instruments back to make room for the contest. "It's always a pleasure to gather with you." The crowd clapped. "So many hungry faces!" The crowd milled, taking in the assortment of costumes.

"Please," the person at the microphone continued, "clear the center of the room so we can begin." The spotlight made the speaker's skin glow, resulting in an almost blinding brilliance.

Sensing the beginnings of a headache, Sharon averted her eyes from the MC. The crowd pushed to the edges of the room, revealing an intricate carving in the center of the dance floor. A series of huge circles confined runes of some sort.

A clock chimed from somewhere in the heart of the place, its tone reverberating through Sharon's solar plexus.

The speaker's beautiful face stretched into a flattering smile. "Time to welcome some fresh blood to this place!" A violinist strode onstage, dressed like a Revolutionary War Soldier. When he placed the bow to the strings, the music enthralled with sweet, yearning notes. The soldier paced behind the speaker, a small shadow that enhanced the speaker's grandeur.

"William Mathison," the speaker threw arms high. The violinist's song picked up in pace as a welcome as the young man stepped onto the stage. Dressed as a police officer, the young man turned and shook his bottom toward the whooping crowd.

The speaker licked pouting lips and tapped long fingers against the microphone. "Very nice, William. Please stand on the first star." One of those long fingers pointed to the decorated floor where a spotlight illuminated a star. While William took a 5, exiting stairwell at the far edge of the stage, the speaker called another name. A cat suited dancer followed William's lead to a star of his own. Two contestants climbed the stairs together, a pair of cow hands complete with boots, hats, and lassos.

131

"Chyna Cameratta," the speaker called, and Chyna took her time ascending, sheepish about the tight skirt and her clumsiness. She showed her fangs, and the crowd cheered. She blushed and waved Sharon's sweatshirt, still clutched in her left hand. She took equal care with the descent, careful not to stumble.

As each contestant took their position, Sharon's discomfort intensified. The contestants grew unnaturally still when they stood on their designated marks. She didn't want her friend to take her place in their circle. Worse, something in the surrounding crowd felt predatory, as though the thinnest of leashes kept a wild pack from attacking.

She squirmed through the crowd to reach Chyna when she reached the bottom of the stairwell. Shaking, she grabbed Chyna's arm and tugged. "We have to go now."

"I can't." Tears stood in Chyna's eyes.

"A stupid costume contest doesn't matter. Seriously, hurry."

Chyna tried to pull away, but Sharon kept her grip on the smaller girl. She dragged Chyna toward the exit.

The speaker's distinctive voice shot fear through her. "Do we have a late entrant?"

All attention - and a literal spotlight - fell on Chyna and Sharon. The girls froze in place. "So, this is how a deer feels when it sees a car's headlights," Sharon thought bleakly before she opted to run. With all her might, she pulled Chyna, who for a little lady seemed to weigh an absolute ton.

Members of the crowd sidled toward the exit, forming an impenetrable wall of humanity.

The speaker's amplified voice cooed. "Now, now. You signed up for this, didn't you, Chyna?"

Chyna whimpered. Her head drooped.

Sweat broke out all over Sharon, her shallow breathing and tingling muscles poised. "Trapped," she thought.

"And we'd be glad to add your friend to the festivities." As the speaker announced this, the crowd made way for the flapper, red pen and sign-up sheet supported by a silver salver.

When the woman neared, Sharon raised her voice in the unnatural quiet that followed the speaker's invitation. "No! Thanks anyway. We have to leave."

The flapper extended the salver, seeming reluctant to approach the open dance floor. Sharon glanced down and noticed the strange symbols on the floor gleamed red under the heat of the spotlight. Red as blood.

The other costume contestants, rooted to their stars, moaned. They grew pale as death and held their hands parallel to the floor. From their wrists dripped blood, though how they'd been cut, Sharon hadn't noticed. Diminutive, twisted creatures clamored from within the innermost circle of the floor's design and, chittering like insects to one another, collected the blood in open, sharp-toothed mouths and in stone bowls.

Sharon's grasp on Chyna's small wrist grew slick, and both girls cried out when they noticed blood hemorrhaging from beneath Sharon's fingers.

Three of the stick-thin creatures that had emerged from the floor sidled, jerking and halting, with their bowls to collect Chyna's blood.

Sharon screamed, spinning until her skirts billowed. The tiny bells sewn into the fabric tinkled.

The three creatures screeched and dropped their bowls to cover their ears.

"She signed up," the flapper drawled.

"Get away from us!" Sharon exaggerated her movements to keep her skirts ringing. She kept the creatures and the flapper before her and backed toward the exit, thinking hopefully, "Maybe the bells will keep the crowd away, too."

No such luck, though. Members of the crowd grabbed Sharon, pulled Chyna from her, and pushed Chyna onto her face while detaining Sharon. Sharon kicked, punched, and bit her detainers.

The three creatures converged on Chyna. She pushed to her knees and yelled Sharon's name as she threw the sweatshirt to her friend.

"Run! Get out of here!"

Tears slicked her face as the creatures manhandled her bleeding wrists into position above the bowls.

Sharon broke free and caught the sweatshirt. She continued to careen forward and caught her friend about the waist. The bells on her skirts made the creatures fall back, and the apparent madness of her wild features won a hasty opening in the crowd. With a strength born of desperation, she carried Chyna like a football tucked under one arm. She drove through the crowd, swiping and punching any who blocked her exit. Even the bouncer stepped back, a half-smile on his lips. Through the intersection, up the street, away from the Crossroads Inn she rushed, Chyna an unconscious ragdoll.

At the bus stop, she settled Chyna on the bench. She wrapped one of Chyna's bleeding wrists with the sweatshirt. She ripped layers of the belly dancing skirting for the other and applied pressure with her palms.

"Please," Sharon prayed. "Help."

Amazingly, a bus pulled up and opened its doors.

Sharon repeated her words, nearly faint with relief.

Aggie the bus driver leaped to help. "What happened?" She didn't wait for an explanation, just helped load Chyna onboard and drove to the hospital ER while Sharon repeated her prayer with every heartbeat.

At the ER, Aggie waited with Sharon while doctors and nurses tended Chyna. Only the television mounted in the corner of the crowded waiting room spilled sound into the stillness. Everyone stared, zombie-like, at the glowing box, waiting for treatment or word about someone receiving treatment. An evening entertainment show played, and Sharon peripherally registered that she recognized the singer announced as the latest 'big thing.' He smiled into the camera as he crooned a catchy tune.

Hours later, a doctor explained they'd stitched Chyna's wounds, but she would be kept for at least a 48-hour mental health evaluation.

Sharon sagged with relief. "She didn't try to kill herself, though."

The doctor looked doubtful. "Sorry. It's procedure."

Aggie tapped the side of Sharon's thigh. "Let's get you back to your dorm." She yawned and stretched. "I'm glad I didn't have any other passengers on the bus when I came to get you." She moved her neck from side to side, working out the kinks of non-movement. "I wasn't scheduled to get to the Crossroads stop for another half hour."

Sharon shuddered at the name.

Aggie put an arm around the student. "Something told me to be early."

The sun rose, a glorious display of gold, orange, and red, to welcome All Saint's Day.

Sadie Hawkins Day

The women transformed the Bessemer Fire Hall Number Three into a feminine fantasy.

Lace as white as bleached bone and hearts of bloody hew dangled and decorated every surface.

"The girls sure should have fun running the race and catching their beaus!" old lady Magill said with a wise smile.

"Sadie Hawkins' Day is always such fun!" said Mrs. Thornbee, whose teenage daughter planned to run the race and catch her "groom" for the evening.

Most of the young people arranged their race positions so that girlfriends caught boyfriends. The Thornbee girl had an arrangement with Tobie McKinnison. They would run for a bit, but he promised to let her catch him. In return, she promised him a kiss when she did.

The women stilled when Hattie strolled through with a cut-glass punch bowl of pink lemonade. Though well into her thirtieth year, Hattie Collins ran the race every year since her teens. She donned a fancy dress and put ribbons in her hair like a caricature of the younger girls. She ran, face reddening with the effort, but the potential beaus always fled faster.

Hattie lived as the embodiment of the spinster, the very reason for Sadie Hawkins day.

Her virtues of hard work and willing spirit were eclipsed by buck teeth and knobby knees. She resembled the old-time comic strip characters.

Even more scandalous, the townsfolk suspected the local water witches had trained Hattie in their magical ways, but they hadn't confirmation.

"Hattie, dear," newly married Millie Charleston said, putting a hand on Hattie's skeletal shoulder, "Are you really going to run again this year?"

Hattie blinked eyes as dark as pitch. "Of course I'm running. I intend on catchin' one this year."

"And what are you going to do once you catch him?"

"What I'm supposed to do, silly."

Mille cleared her throat. "Hattie, haven't you noticed the men run harder from you than from the other ladies? Maybe it's time to give up."

Hattie cocked her head to the left, a crooked smile cracking her face. "Why'd I do that?"

Millie sighed and shook her head. She walked away in bemused disgust. "Don't say I didn't warn you," she muttered.

The time for the race arrived. Young girls lined up behind young men, all dressed for the dance to follow. Jibes and encouragements, whistles and catcalls filled the air.

The Mayor of Canine Acres tugged at his bolero tie and cleared his throat for quiet.

"Ladies and gentlemen, thank you for attending the eightieth running of the Sadie Hawkins Race!"

Those assembled applauded and whooped their enthusiasm. "Please remember, gentlemen, if a lady captures you, you are her date for the dance." Another eruption of fervor.

"As always, Reverend Brown will be on-hand if'n you crazy young people want to get hitched."

He waggled his eyebrows, and the crowd chortled. "Thank you to the more senior ladies of the town for preparing a wonderful feast and suitably tricked-out dance hall. Music will be provided by our own Backwater Boys."

The crowd offered polite applause, but the racers shifted anxiously.

The Mayor cleared his throat and adjusted his tie. "So, without further ado, the race begins as my gun fires. Three, two, one…"

The report of the gun cut through the early evening air with a crack. The racers set off with squeals. Several men slowed for capture by their chosen dates. They fell into giggling hugs and progressed to the converted dance hall. Other men sprinted just outside of the ladies' grasp, taunting and teasing.

Otis Adams, still smelling of military duty and a new Master's Degree from the local State University, looked over his shoulder. Surprise registered on his handsome face. Hattie Collins pumped her skinny legs and arms in hot pursuit. Her smile appeared maniacal, and single-minded. An obsessive look glowed in her eyes.

"Shoot. Just like the old days," he thought, and poured on some speed. Technically, he'd aged out of the race, but the matrons raised such a clamor for his participation that he laughingly agreed. "What could it hurt?" Of course, he didn't realize Hattie still ran.

For years, he'd sought an escape from his one-time schoolmate. In his panic, his breathing became labored. With single-minded focus, she homed in on him like a locked missile. He took a deep breath and made the corner. He knew the end rope of the race meant safety.

"Why did I agree to this?" He huffed, regretting how far he'd allowed his muscles to go from boot camp. "I left this po-dunk town to get away from this hillbilly nonsense!"

But, his mother and aunt insisted, "It will be fun! Just go. Allow some pretty girl to catch you."

"But what about Hattie?"

They'd reassured him, "She's getting too old to run, poor dear."

"I'm the same age that she is."

"It's different for men. Ya'all age better or somethin'. Now let some pretty young thing catch you."

He glanced over his shoulder to find Hattie'd closed the gap. "Pretty young thing? My tired butt!" He curled his upper lip and pushed his legs to carry him further faster.

The other racers fell away in couples or the men crossed the safety line. The crisp November air felt colder and thinner in the mountains.

"I can get there," he thought. "Not much different from boot camp, right?"

He felt Hattie's fingertips brush his shoulders and panicked.

"Run, man!" He willed his muscles to life.

Her fingernails scratched him. He remembered this run from his formative years. Hattie always pursued him. She even haunted some of his dreams as an adult, a menacing force in pursuit, wishing to take his freedom. "Would it really be so bad to go to a dance with her?"

Her yellowed buck teeth surrounded by smudged purplish lipstick resembled a donkey's mouth.

"Yep. It would be. Can't do it." The world began to spin. His knees weakened.

"What the heck?" A black fog closed off his peripheral vision. His stomach lurched, and he stumbled.

"Adams, are you okay?" Hattie drawled. Her face twisted with concern.

He didn't answer, just dropped off to oblivion.

When he came to, Hattie loomed over him, absurd pink ribbons tying pigtails framing her gaunt face. He felt hung-over and groggy.

"What happened?"

"Shhh, you're okay now." Hattie placed a cool rag on his forehead. He meant to swipe it away, but his arms would not cooperate.

"What is going on?"

"I finally caught you is what's going on." Her face looked like a malformed jack-o-lantern in the low light. She fidgeted. "I need to ask. Will you be marryin' me today?"

He recoiled and reacted with a harsh laugh. "Marrying you? Why on earth would I do that?"

Her eyebrows raised. "Well, ya needn't be so mean about it, ya know. I guess I'll just have to go ahead with my plan."

"Plan? What plan?"

She ignored him.

He turned his head, expecting to see the dance hall or a doctor's office. He lay on a cot in a wooden room. The wall resembled the wad and stick designs of old-time cabins. Dark red stained the knotty pine floor.

"Where am I?"

"Home."

Pain flashed behind his eyes. He shook his head to clear his thoughts. He smelled chemicals like cleaning fluid and something else. His head ached and his heart pounded against his sore ribs. He tried to wipe his mouth, but again his arms wouldn't react because strips of white, lacy material bound his wrists to the sides of the cot. It scratched his skin as he pulled.

"Legs must be bound, too," he realized. He tried his chest and hips. Unmovable.

"Why am I tied up?"

"Can't have you runnin' off ag'in, now kin I?" She giggled and batted her eyelashes.

He scoped out the cabin again. Double bolts secured the door. The only window's shutters closed out light. A small farm-house buffet sat beneath the window. The fragile beauty of a white magnolia blossom floating in a mason jar looked out of place among worn farm tools set atop. Wooden shelves lined two of the walls, their contents hidden by shadows and spider webs.

Hattie collected a cauldron, some mason jars, and twine-bound herbs from the shelves. She paused to regard a spider's work. With a spring in her step, she bounded to the table and set the items among the farming implements. She hummed a reel, her feet tapping the time.

A tallow candle smelled nicer than the rue she set aflame. He wrinkled his nose and turned his face away.

"Aren't we supposed to go to the dance? I mean, isn't that why we run that stupid race?"

She turned from her task to smile wide. "The race ain't stupid, and we'll go the dance in a bit."

"Can you let me sit up, please? This isn't very comfortable."

"In good time. In good time." She resumed humming and added ingredients from the mason jars.

"What are you doing over there?"

"Makin' a stayin' potion. Now that I caught ya, I intend on keepin' ya."

"A potion? Keeping? Hattie, this doesn't make sense. You do know that there is no real magic, right?"

"Is that what they taught you at yer city schools?" She swished her skirts as she stirred into the cauldron some dried flower petals.

He strained against the bindings again.

She shrugged, "Well, I've been learnin' too. The Mountain Grannies are my teachers."

His eyes widened. *"Mountain Grannies? Witch Doctors, Dowsers, and Snake Salesman."*

"Seriously?" He felt a wave of cold run through him. He'd forgotten the local superstitions.

Since many of the local residents were universally poor or not traditionally employed, modern medical care remained beyond their reach. So, they turned to folk remedies provided by Mountain Grannies and their ilk. The superstitious people believed in their magic and treated them with respect and fear.

"Stupid, ignorant fools!" He hated this place. Sweat trickled all over his skin, despite the weather's growing chill. Hattie ground something with a pestle in a wooden mortar bowl. "She's not scaring me."

Yet he shuddered. He struggled against his bindings without effect. Pouring as much authority into his voice as the current indignity allowed, he said, "Hattie, this is enough. Let me go. Now."

She approached holding a metal funnel and the small metal cauldron. She rested a gentle hand on his forehead. Malicious humor danced along her wrinkled lips.

"Sorry. You don't get to say a thing until this day is over. Today's all about us girls." The low light pushed her eyes further into her pale, thin face, lending to her skeletal aspect. She positioned the funnel over his mouth.

He pressed his lips tight, like a toddler rejecting a meal.

"Now, don't be that way," she cooed.

She set the funnel on his chest and pinched his nose.

He writhed, trying to dislodge the funnel. It fell to the ground, but she barked out a braying laugh and continued to pinch his nose.

He needed a breath. His brain fogged, and rather than black out, he stole a quick gasp.

Ready, she poured the foul-smelling, gloppy contents of the cauldron down his throat.

He spit, but she continued to pour. He struggled, but though some oozed over his lips, down his chin, and into his nose. Some slid down his throat.

"That's good." She ran a hand through his close-cropped hair before she resumed her nose pinch. Some muddy liquid squelched from his nostrils.

"You're going to drown me," he sputtered and struggled.

She ignored him and poured.

He worked his tongue to push the dirt-tasting bitterness from his mouth, and despite his best efforts, he swallowed some more. It slid like boogers down his throat, and his stomach complained. Where the glop touched his skin, it numbed like Novocain.

"The funnel would've been tidier." She wiped his mouth with a dishrag.

He pumped his fists, pulling and relaxing, pulling and relaxing in subtle movements, slow, controlled muscle isolations he hoped would not attract her attention but would loosen his bounds. *"I have to get out of here."* His movements slowed as the drunk feeling returned. Rational thought grew difficult.

She restored the pot and grasped a vial with a dropper.

"Most water witches don't teach this kinda stuff." She motioned toward the table. "They stick to cures and the like. But Grandy Thaxton's been to the Big Easy. That's New Orleans. She has some good friends there."

Hattie shook two large beetles from an insect house into the mortar and crushed them with a stone pestle. She tipped it toward him as she worked. Their thin stick legs thrashed as she crushed their bodies.

She reached and yanked some hairs from his head. He winced.

She plucked a couple of her own mousey strands as well and muttered gibberish words.

"This is stupid. Kidnapping. Let me go, Hattie, before you're arrested." He put as much vehemence and authority as he could into his slurred voice. The hairs on his arm stood on end, betraying gooseflesh.

The air thickened with electricity. The feeling of bugs crawled over his chilled skin, and he shivered.

She dropped a clear oil into the corners of his eyes. It bit and brought tears.

146

She returned to the buffet and set the cauldron over the candle. Foul smells drifted with eddies of swirling dust. His neck and shoulder muscles tensed. His stomach gave a heave, but his esophagus wouldn't help his eject. His heavy eyelids drooped, but he forced himself awake.

She opened a lid on a dark-glass jar and removed an inflated puffer fish. She kissed the spiny creature, then turned it to 'kiss' him on the cheek.

"Kiss kiss," she said with a cackling giggle. The thing struggled in her grasp, mouth gasping.

Her tear-filled cow brown gaze bored into his drooping eyes. "I've always loved you," she whispered. "I know you know that." She bent to kiss his lips with her rough, chapped ones. Her breath stunk of ramps.

He choked.

She returned to the table where she used a thrashing knife to cut the fish into slivers thin enough to see through. Her knife skills impressed him, despite himself.

His heart thrilled as he pulled his hand free of the loosened bindings. Using this hard-won freedom, he worked with watchful, quiet movements at the ties holding his torso. His leaden lids slid, further obscuring observations.

She chanted or sang, something plodding and without harmony. A thick, foul-smelling smoke wafted from the cauldron and clouded the room. She swayed like a snake caught in a charmer's spell.

His feeling of being drunk intensified. "I've got to get out of here," he slurred. His hand loosened the body bindings. He reached across his body to free his opposite hand.

"To heck with careful. She's crazy." He fumbled and fought with the ropes for his liberty. He sat up to untie his feet.

Thump.

The knife that she used to cut the ingredients reverberated on the table, skewering his hand.

Shock prevented an immediate reaction. His mouth and eyes flew open. He screamed from pain. She continued to chant while she pushed his head back. That she'd speared his hand didn't faze her. She took a wire and retied his uninjured hand and put a wide leather belt around his forehead, securing him to the cot.

"She's a skinny bitch. I outweigh her by at least 50 pounds. Why can't I fight her off?"

His head buzzed and ached. His hand throbbed. Wooziness intensified.

She held a large sewing needle threaded with wide, waxed twine. She set it on the cot beside him. She blew a hand filled with grub-white powder into his face.

He thrashed and gagged.

Her laughter echoed from the wooden walls. It reverberated within his aching head. The world swirled, colors blending, traces of passage like phantoms luring him to sleep.

***

"Reverend, we want to be hitched." Hattie wore a bit of lace over her braided hair.

The reverend leaned forward, his brow cratered with confusion. "Is this so, Otis?"

Though he strained against the action, Otis Adams could do nothing more than nod.

If he did well here, Hattie'd cut the stitches that held his inner lips and tongue together. Her skill with the needle impressed him. Not many people could produce tiny, effective stitches through skin with thick, waxed twine. When he looked in the mirror, he couldn't detect the stitching unless he curled his lips up, which pulled and burned.

The reverend wiped sweat from his brow with his back pocket handkerchief. "Where've you two been? We ain't seen you in these parts for about a year now." He stuffed the cloth back into his faded jeans' pocket. "Not since last Sadie Hawkins, I reckon."

"A year? Woo-ee," she said, draped over Otis' arm. "We've been about. Just making preparations for the weddin', ya know?"

She giggled and buried her face in Ottis' arm.

Otis stared straight before him, blinking back regret.

She continued, "We don't need no big ceremony, just somethin' private. Heck, we'd even jump a broom!" She cackled at her joke.

The Reverend touched Otis' arm. "You feelin' okay, son? You look a bit out of it."

Otis did not react. He thought of the voodoo doll crafted in his image, hidden in her garter. *"She can hurt me using that doll. Has, in fact."*

Hattie chimed in. "Oh, he's jist fine. Jist fine. My Otis is going to make me the happiest bride these parts has ever seen. Isn't that right, Otis?"

Otis gulped and nodded.

From Grandma's House

The monster in this story stretched a trap one frigid Thanksgiving evening, ready for the unwary traveler. Camouflaged, it resembled safe passage, the familiar route home.

However, when traversing over the river, many people forgot bridges remained unfortified by earthen warmth. Through the woods, snow drifted.

Glutted on culinary goodness, stuffed with tryptophan and digesting carbs, heavy-eyed drivers eased their seatbelts over struggling stretchy pants. In the back seat of the family vehicle, toddlers' heads tumbled to rest against complaining siblings' shoulders. Teens disconnected into air bud escapes. Sleepy spouses encouraged concord, yawning while imparting wisdom.

Headlights revealed nothing of concern, yet once they stumbled upon the trap, the monster spun them, seized control of their progress, rendered them powerless to slow or stop. It relished the squeal of the auto's wheels. The screams of the passengers sounded like songs to the black ice. With appreciation, how the wind blew!

*Over the River and through the woods to Grandmother's house we go!
The horse knows the way to carry the sleigh
Through the wide and drifting snow-o!
Over the river and through the woods, oh how the wind does blow!"

All I Want for Christmas

Ed silently cursed the biting winter wind gusting through his hiding place. Without its foliage, the maple tree offered little protection from the elements. Earlier in the year, the branch just outside Beth's window provided the perfect combination of excellent view and camouflage. Beth kept her blinds up to catch the early morning sunrise, and a nightlight on her bedside stand offered enough illumination to watch her while she slept.

She also enjoyed a crisp breeze, so she kept her window unlatched and sometimes open.

Ed discovered the excellent vantage provided by the window in autumn, when his flame-bright hair blended with the maple's vibrant leaves. He'd followed Beth home after the first day of their sophomore year, when she'd shown him kindness. As the new kid in the district, Ed struggled to find his classes. Beth noticed and assisted. She even offered him a seat next to hers during the lunch period, where she introduced him to her friends.

They sat together every lunch period thereafter, and before a week's conclusion, Ed knew Beth's schedule better than his own. He offered to carry her books, which she refused with a laugh and a playful swat to his arm. "I can carry my own books, silly."

Almost from that first day, Ed knew. Along with her sweet and helpful nature, her pretty face and ready good humor won his heart.

His all-consuming goal since that day was to win her heart in return.

He'd set a personal goal. Beth would love him by Christmas.

That level of commitment required some significant work. He wanted to enchant her. Woo her. Win her.

He listened intently to her conversations. Her voice resonated within him. He learned her likes and aversions. He celebrated her victories, such as passed tests, and commiserated when things didn't go as she hoped. He offered to "take care of" some mean girls who made her feel bad, channeling his best gangsta, which made her giggle, sniff away her sadness, and say, "Thanks. You made me feel better."

He contemplated her every move, learning her daily schedules outside of school. He knew which families employed her to babysit. He knew when she walked her pet poodle, Snookums. He grew concerned when, one Saturday afternoon, her cousin Gina allowed her to drive her car in the nearby mall parking lot.

The thought of Beth driving away doubled Ed's resolve.

He investigated her most private sanctum. While she babysat one Sunday afternoon, he scaled the tree and snuck in to inventory her things. She favored blue and light, spring-like colors. Silver jewelry dangled from her neck and wrists and glinted in her childhood ballerina music box. She painted every fingernail, worn sporty-short, different colors and kept the polishes in a bag under the sink in her ensuite bathroom. Her favorite singer designed the perfume she spritzed on her wrist and neck. She wore a size ten or a medium, bought her underthings at the pink bag store, and she secretly read racy romance novels which she hid between her mattress and box springs.

Her menstrual cycle began during the second week of every month.

Christmas approached, and with it the school's winter break.

Ed had the information he needed. From his careful observations, he knew Beth's weakness and strengths. This break, he'd "happen" upon her. He'd ask her out on a date. He'd woo and win her for his own.

And if she didn't come easily, Ed knew how best to subdue the object of his affection. He had a hidden room in his basement designed to look just like her bedroom, from its Himalayan salt lamp to its pastel floral duvet. He'd decorated it with a white Christmas tree and soundproof walls. He'd even stuffed a bit of steamy reading material between the mattress and box spring, though he hoped she'd find enacting the real thing more interesting.

She should feel right at home in the room he designed for her. The only missing element would be a window with a maple tree outside, but in his basement, she wouldn't need one.

Besides, they wouldn't want anyone else peeking in on Beth once she'd relocated to his heart.

Let it Snow

The happy couple snuggled beneath a soft blanket, backs to the sofa, toes warming in the fireplace's glow. They cupped oversized mugs of steaming hot cocoa, marshmallows melting within. She placed her head on his shoulder with a contented sigh. He kissed the crown of her head, inhaling the coconut of her shampoo.

Neither lover listened to the symphonic storm raging outside their humble abode.

"I'll put another log on the fire." He set his cup aside and shrugs out of their cocoon. "Wow, it's really coming down! I can't even see the mailbox anymore."

She joined him at the window above the woodbin. "That's a lot of snow!" She widened her eyes. "Thank goodness we don't have anywhere to go."

When he removed a log from the bin, something fast and brown and furry scurried from the pile, making a beeline for his feet. He yelled, dancing out of the way of the rampaging rodent, heedless of his surroundings. He careened into his much smaller girlfriend, knocking her aside.

She windmilled her arms, stumbling over her fluffy socks. With a sickening crunch, she slammed the back of her head onto the mantle. Blood bloomed brighter than the poinsettia she'd displayed on the buffet table. Her eyes fluttered closed before her body thumped to the hearth.

The wild interloper forgotten, he fell to his knees at her side. "Babe!" He drew her to his chest, cradling her head like a newborn's. "Please wake up." His lower lip trembled as he brushed a swath of hair from her eyes.

She moaned and reached for her head. "What happened?"

He swiped his eyes and cleared his throat. "You fell." He stroked her hair. His hand came away sticky with blood. "Shit! You're bleeding!" He released her to run into the bathroom and return with a towel to staunch the flow.

When he applied pressure, she gasped. "It really hurts." Her pupils didn't match, one enlarged, the other a pinprick.

"I think you have a concussion." He rushed for the coats. "I better get you to the hospital."

"But it's terrible outside." Her voice drifted.

"I'll have to drive slow." He helped her with her scarf and handed her mittens. "Keep pressure on that towel. I'll warm up the car and come back in a couple of minutes, ok?"

She nodded, but the movement elicited a battle with nausea.

When he opened the door, cold swept into their little dwelling as though anxious to check on the patient. She retrieved the blanket and wrapped it around her shoulders.

With another wintery burst, he returned. "Okay, let's go."

"I don't feel so good." She wobbled when she bent to slip into her boots.

"Don't fall again, babe!" He slipped an arm around her and pulled her to him.

The wind sang, baring a swirl of silver and white reflecting porchlight glow. The precipitation assaulted their faces. A gust pushed him off-balance. He struggled for purchase on the icy walkway, but when he fell, he pulled her with him. He jammed his elbow to break the fall, but her reaction time lagged. She struck the side of her head and lost consciousness for the second time that evening.

The storm picked up, as though hoping to bury the lovers beneath a crystalline blanket it devised. He crawled to use the house as a support for him to stand. With tiny, shuffling steps, arms outstretched like a newly ambulating babe, he reached his gal.

"Baby, get up. Please!"

She didn't respond.

"I don't think I can carry you. You have to get up."

No reaction.

"Great." He glared at the laden clouds. His lips chapped as he licked them, thinking of the best way to get her to their running car. He opted to scoop her up by her shoulders and drag her. Her head lolled like a rag doll's, but he reached the car. He set her against his legs as he twisted to open the door and heave her in.

Along the pathway to the vehicle, he left the blanket she'd wrapped herself in and the towel. He fastened her seatbelt and closed the car door.

The snow had accumulated despite the running defrosters, but he decided to chance it. He activated the windshield wipers to clear a view, put the car in gear, and began the journey.

Ice formed a barrier between the asphalt and the tires. Snow disguised the problem. As though the elements conspired against the couple, his car slid when they reached the first stop sign. The vehicle cruised through the intersection.

He panicked and pressed the brake with desperation. "Sweet mother…" His fingers squeezed the steering wheel, uselessly rigid.

The car picked up uncontrolled speed as it careened over a hill.

The neighbor's large picture window displayed a scene of Rockwellian comfort, with a family toasting mountain pies in their fireplace.

She woke when he screamed and threw his hands over his face. With a shattering of picture window and twisting of Detroit's best steel, the uncontrolled car crashed the neighbor's party.

Yule Cat

Wind whipped through the valley like an avenging spirit, pulling at Bettina's package, tugging her inadequate coat, and with a 'whoosh,' stealing her knitted cap. Although she scrambled after it, the wind outstripped her. She imagined the breezes shook with giggles as she noted her hat's tumbling progress.

Bettina's eyes watered from the cold and the loss, but she pressed her lips together, ducked her head, and pushed on to her home where her two young boys waited. The mere thought of them brought warmth to her despite the chilled weather.

Outside of their door, she straightened her hair, took a deep breath, and plastered a smile across her otherwise exhausted face. As she did every night she worked, she knocked to announce her arrival to prevent startling her boys. "I'm home! Happy Christmas Eve, my darlings!"

The boys rushed her with the enthusiasm of puppies, bouncing around her with embraces and tales of their daily adventures. She kissed the tops of each of their heads, and the cares of the workday melted away. All the last-minute shoppers with their unreasonable demands and their entitled attitudes drowned in the boys' choruses.

"Mrs. Schwartz gave us peppermints. See!" The youngest, Johann, held up a candy cane sucked to a sticky, white point.

"Yum!" she laughed.

"She said she's sorry she had to leave, but her son is coming, and she had to baste the turkey." Tommin, the oldest by a year and a half, puffed out his chest. "But I told her I could take care of everything until you got home. And I did!"

"You certainly did, my splendid boy!"

"I helped," Johann pouted.

"Of course you did, darling." Bettina ruffled his hair.

"Look. We wrapped our presents for you. See? They're here, under the tree." Tommin pointed into the shared space of their tiny dwelling while he pulled her toward the straggly pine tree with its handmade decorations. "Sit here. You must be tired. Was it very busy at the shops today? Mrs. Schwartz reckoned it would be." He guided her to the only chair in the room. "I made some chocolate milk. Would you like some?"

"You must take a breath between your questions so I can answer," Bettina laughed.

Johann clambered onto her lap and extended his candy cane. "You can have some of my peppermint if you want, Momma. I only licked the top part once."

"No, no, you enjoy it." She kissed his sugary lips and sighed. "We have to get ready for church. Go and change. I'll just rest my eyes a minute." Her eyelids slid closed like a curtain after its final act.

Tommin pulled Johann from her lap. "We'll be super quick."

The cuckoo clock that hung over their sturdy little table announced the time, startling Bettina from her doze. "Good Heavens, we've got to hurry, or we'll be late." She retrieved her bag which had slipped to the floor beside the chair during the enthusiastic greeting, stashed it under the tree skirt she'd knitted before Tommin's birth, and splashed water onto her face at the kitchen sink.

The boys bickered in their shared bedroom until she called for them. With some jostling for position, they arrived, two bedraggled but enthusiastic soldiers awaiting inspection. Bettina ran the dish cloth over Johann's sticky face and flattened Tommin's wayward "Alfalfa sprout" hair with a splash of water and her fingers. "You look so handsome." She embraced them both, inhaling their little boy scents of peppermint and mischief. "I'm sorry I couldn't get you new outfits, though."

"It's okay, Momma. God don't care what we're wearing."

Johann nodded. "And new clothes itch."

"When I was a little girl, my momma, your grandmother, would always buy me a new outfit for Christmas Eve." Bettina's eyes misted, and she sniffed. "She used to say you had to have brand new clothes, or the Yule Cat would eat you up."

Johann stuck out his chin, color rising in his cheeks. "Da used to say Gram was crazy."

"Different cultures, that's all. She wasn't crazy. It was a tale from the old country, from when your Grandmother was a little girl."

"Besides, who cares what Da said." Tommin's lower lip jutted out in a perfect pout. "He's not here to help us."

Bettina knelt and pulled them into another embrace. "It's not his fault. You know that. The good Lord called him home is all." She kissed them each on their chubby cheeks. "Now put on your coats and mufflers. Gloves and hats, too. It's cold out there, and we have a long walk to get to church."

"Not too long." Tommin wrapped his neck with a red scarf and slid a black and tan knitted cap onto his head. "School's a block further."

"That's true. I forgot what a seasoned traveler you are, my brave first and second graders!"

Properly outfitted for the weather, they held hands as they trooped into the windy night.

"Momma, you forgotted your hat!" Johann pointed to her knotting-in-the wind hair.

"The wind liked it so much, it stole mine!"

Johann giggled, but Tommin frowned. He swiped his from his head. "Here, take mine."

"No, no! I've got a lot of hair to keep my ears warm. I don't want yours to get too cold and fall off!" They all giggled as Tommin replaced his cap.

Their merry conversation ended when a growl rumbled from a side street. The three froze in place, eyes wide and reflecting the streetlights' glow. The boys squeezed their mother's hands. Tommin whispered, "What was that?"

Bettina licked her chapped lips and turned to face the repeated sound. From the gloom of the alley, the lithe form of a vast, snowy mountain lion padded on enormous, silent paws. It peeled back its lips in the most unfriendly smile, its long fangs curving and sharp.

"Well, well, well. What have we here? Travelers this Yule season, and without the protection of new clothes."

"You've got to be kidding me," Bettina breathed.

The nightmarish creature hulked toward them, fearsome claws retracting into paws larger than stop signs, its corpse-white eyes locked on its prey.

Bettina stepped in front of her boys, shielding them with her thin form as best she could. Even with the bulk of her puffy winter coat, though, the boys remained visible to the beast.

Its voice rumbled, a thunderous roar, "Step aside, woman. I will have my feast."

Bettina's face reddened and her nostrils flared. "Are you kidding me?"

The rumbling cat purred, "It's the rules. Any child not smelling of fresh fibers is consumed."

"Not here, in this land." Bettina squared her shoulders. "Not now. Certainly not tonight." Anger flashed in her eyes. "And absolutely not my boys."

She strode toward the beast, an enraged Valkyrie, swollen with indignation.

"I've never heard of a more dreadful being in my life. Despicable! Here we are, scraping together what little we have to feed ourselves, and you're going to try to eat us because we don't have new clothes? I think not! Talk about oppressing the poor!"

The mammoth cat shook its head. "I don't think that's the intent…"

"I work my fingers to the bones to care for my boys. I slave at two different jobs since my husband's death. Not a soul except my neighbor helps us. We don't take from the government. We don't ask for much at all. But I'll be DAMNED if I allow some decrepit, old legend to stalk out of the shadows and try to shame us!"

She poked her pointing index finger in the enormous cat's face.

"Do I make myself clear?"

The great legend, the bugaboo from ages and lands past, looked abashed. It lowered its head and flexed its front claws, left then right, left then right, kneading holes into the concrete.

"I asked, did I make myself clear?"

The beast's great tale swished low to the ground. "It's tradition."

"It was. Long ago. But not anymore. Not here. Not my sons." Despite Bettina's diminutive stature, she seemed to tower over the beast. "Do you understand?"

The Yule Cat's tongue snuck between its cloudy gray lips. "Yes, Ma'am."

"Fine, then." Bettina straightened her puffy winter coat, turned to her boys who rushed to grab her gloved hands, and marched toward church. "Merry Christmas to you, Cat."

"Happy Yule to you," the Cat replied.

Wendigo Wood

Billy followed his father into the wintery woods, but his heart beat an erratic percussion and his gaze flitted faster than a pond could turn to ice. Powdery snow flurried. Songless birds hopped in the snow-slicked branches. Billy chewed his lips, a problem that resulted in chapping which in turn inspired him to chew his lips. He always forgot the lip balm his mother bought for him, just as he always forgot the stretchy superhero gloves she insisted he carry in his parka's pocket.

He stole a glance over his shoulder, as much to see how far they'd ventured into the trees as to reassure himself their footprints in the snow marked their escape route, should it come to that.

"Daddy," he said, the cold wind reducing his word to a whisper, "are we almost there?"

His father chuckled and rested a heavily gloved hand on the top of Billy's tousled-capped head. "Haven't got to the stand of evergreens yet. Do you see a Christmas tree candidate here?"

"No." Billy clutched his father's hand and ignored the sensation of being watched. A wave of trembles shot up his spine. "Daddy, how'd you hear of this place?"

"Heard some guys at work talking about it. Said this here's the best place to get a fresh tree." His father guided the six-year-old through the sparkling afternoon, whistling "Oh Tannenbaum" as they went. He shouldered a large, leather bag with two axes, a hand saw, and twine, and his cell phone clipped to his belt.

Billy worried a flap of skin from his lower lip with his front teeth, thinking, "Daddy's strong. He could even fight off Big Foot if he came after us." He shivered again, though, and nestled closer to his dad's thick legs. That creeping sensation of being watched worried its way through him.

"You're sure it was this woods?"

"It's the only one around, isn't it?"

"No, Peewee and his family go to a 'cut your own' tree farm near their house."

His dad snorted. "You pay through the nose at places like that. This here? This Is God's country. Nobody owns these trees, so we can take anyone you like, and nobody's any the wiser."

Billy's heart pounded as fast and hard as if he'd run in the school's relay races. He touched his chest where the big, silver crucifix his granddad gave to him hung from its chain and said a silent prayer. He didn't like the silence

169

surrounding them. It made their footfalls and Dad's whistles echo.

"Here we are!" His dad dropped his pack to his feet. "Pick our tree."

Clumps of pine trees grew amongst the elms and oaks. Billy suspected something watched from behind their dark green needles, something with ancient, dangerous eyes. The fresh scent of evergreen masked something rotten, a sickly-sweet decay. Billy rubbed his reddened nose and considered the trees from the safety of his dad's shadow.

His dad selected an ax. "Well?"

Billy pointed to a well-shaped conifer of about six feet. He followed when his dad closed on the chosen tree.

"You have to give me a bit of space, kiddo, so I can swing the ax."

Billy lingered, shifting his weight from leg to leg. "You know, maybe we should get a fake tree instead."

"What's going on, Pal?"

Billy shrugged, a movement considerably muted by his padded winter coat. "My friend Chuck has a fake tree, and you can't even tell it's not real unless you touch it."

"I thought we had a plan. Pick our own tree." His dad squatted to look into Billy's eyes. "You won't find a fake tree that smells like these."

The rotting beneath the clean bite of pine burned in Billy's nose. Tears stung his eyes and cooled his cheeks. He sniffed.

"I just want to go home." He stole glances around, feeling as though the trees closed in, an imposing, prickly barrier blocking any retreat. His hair stood on end, certain of corpse-pale eyes hidden nearby. He shook with more than cold. "Please, Daddy."

His dad studied Billy's face, squeezed Billy's arm. He swallowed hard, brow furrowed, lips a firm line.

"Okay." His voice came out as barely a croak. He cleared his throat and glanced up at the sky roiling with dark clouds. "The weather's taking a turn, anyway." He ruffled the top of Billy's knitted cap and stretched his mouth into an uneasy smile.

As if the observation caused the action, the clouds disgorged their chilling precipitation in great, blinding bursts.

Billy hugged his dad.

"Let's get out of here." His dad grabbed his ax and bag with one hand while guiding his son with the other.

A cacophony ripped through the woods, a screeching, inhuman howl that circled with the newly biting wind. Billy fought to keep himself from peeing. He trembled.

"Daddy?"

His dad pulled Billy close, still as a deer listening for a safe direction to flee.

"This way." He pulled Billy with a firm grip on his shoulder. His dad's broad shoulders hunched and his knees bent, the way they did when he boxed. Everything about Billy's father tensed as they fled through the conifers into the wide expanse of deciduous trees that led to their parked Jeep.

A clack, clack, clack, like bones knocking against one another spiraled around them, a hungry laugh accompanied by jagged balls of ice pelting their exposed faces. A screech, a thump, and a tall, gaunt figure landed in front of the father and son. Its fevered eyes sunk deep into a gray-white face, more shadow than plane. It snapped its worn, yellowed teeth at them. Icicle-sharp fingernails tipped hands twisted into claws. The flesh of the thing stretched across a hairless, skeletal figure, the personification of desperation, of deprivation, of starvation itself. It had chewed through its own lips in its fervor, leaving jagged flaps of skin edged with frozen blood, and it wore nothing but an unadorned loincloth and a neck plate of hundreds of fingerbones hollowed out and strung on human-skin leather.

Billy screamed and buried his face in his dad's side.

His dad swung the bag, making contact with the thing's shoulder when it charged. A squelching sound, and Billy's dad grunted and stumbled. Billy whimpered, a pain lancing his bicep, but he most noted his dad's blood gleaming on the thing's thick nails.

With no lips to disguise them, the thing's teeth stretched long, chewing constantly. It lunged and sunk those teeth into the flesh beneath Billy's dad's scarf, staining it with a gush of warm crimson. It dodged Billy's dad's swung bag, clamped onto the forearm, bit until a sickening crunch dragged a scream from Billy and his dad. His dad's arm jutted at an unnatural angle, and he dropped the tool bag.

"No, no, please, no!" Billy pleaded as the thing bit great chunks from his father. The little boy's hand instinctively sought and found the silver crucifix which he pulled from beneath his coat.

"Help," he prayed, tears and an inelegant offering.

But the thing swiped and darted quick and deadly as thought, taking piece after piece of Billy's dad with each attack.

Then, the strongest man Billy knew, his daddy, groaned, fell to his knees, pushed Billy, and hissed, "Run."

Billy stumbled back a few paces, incredulous eyes witnessing the unrelenting horror.

"Run!" Billy's dad slid something across the bloodied, combat-packed snow to Billy. The cell phone, its screen newly cracked and bloodied. Billy scooped it and clutched it to his chest with the crucifix.

The thing continued its attacks.

With the last of his strength, Dad yelled, "Run, damn it, Billy, Run!"

Billy ran. Tree branches swiped his face. He slid over divots and fallen timber and ferns frozen into delicate designs. Billy's feet thundered toward the car, though he didn't know what he'd do once he reached it.

That insane howl pursued him, and Billy darted faster, his heart pounding, his breath gasping aching stabs of cold.

Parked at the woods' tree line, the Jeep offered an ineffectual sort of protection, but the only possible safety available to him. He sprinted when he saw it, but he felt the frozen ground's vibrations as the thing pursued him.

Billy leapt into the driver's seat and slammed the door shut behind him.

The thing, slicked with his father's blood, thumped into the side of the car. Its ribs protruded, as did its collar and hip bones. Its deadly nails scratched at the door's handle, but Billy had locked it. He turned the key in the ignition the way his daddy had many times until the engine roared to life. He dialed the three digits to call the police. 9-1-1.

"Help, please! This thing ate my daddy, and it's trying to get into the car." He screamed and dropped the phone when the thing ran its nails across the glass, gouging four deep tracks.

Billy slid all the way to the edge of the seat and pressed the floor petal on the left, the way daddy did when he put the car in gear. He pulled on the gearshift, but nothing budged.

The thing pounded on the door, pressing its hideous face against the side window.

"Go away," Billy yelled, but the thing scratched and pounded on the door, the roof, the windshield. With a great splintering of glass, the passenger side window shattered. The thing's abnormally long, skeletal arms reached into the vehicle, but Billy scrambled away. He kicked at the attacker, and when it snagged Billy's left leg, Billy stabbed it with the crucifix still clutched in his hand.

The thing screeched and withdrew its hand before Billy could retrieve his cross which had plunged through the thing's palm. It grasped the necklace with its other hand, but with a hiss, it withdrew its ministration. Billy thought he saw wisps of smoke from the thing's palms drifting heavenward.

Billy noticed a knob on the gear shift and pushed it in while pulling the gear shift into drive. He barely reached the petals, but he half squatted at the edge of the seat, half stood to manage the petals and sort of see through the steering wheel. The 9-1-1 operator's voice proclaimed "We've tracked your location. Help is on the way."

Somehow, Billy limped the car to the highway where he met the police near the wood's entry. He burst into relieved tears. "My daddy's still out there. If that thing didn't eat all of him by now. You have to save him!"

They wrapped him with blankets and put pressure on one of Billy's wounds, especially a deep one that burned.

"Kid's in shock," one of the policemen told his partner who radioed for reinforcements and an ambulance. "You think you can tell us what happened, son?"

"You have to shoot it! I stabbed it with my cross, but it took it. It was eating my daddy! Eating him!"

The officers locked eyes for a silent moment.

"Was it a bear?"

"No. A monster." Trembling and tears overtook him.

Additional police cars and an ambulance arrived. A young EMT smiled at Billy. "Let's take a look at these scrapes."

The lead officer organized the new arrivals. "Kid said something ate his dad. You can see the path the kid took, but I'm pretty sure we know where we're heading. Stick together."

The EMT guided the inconsolable Billy aboard the ambulance. "We're going for a ride to the hospital to check out these battle wounds. Hey, Joe?"

The driver answered, "Yeah?"

"Think we can use the sirens? I bet this young man's never been in an ambulance with sirens before."

The EMTs asked questions and talked as they treated Billy's scrapes. He winced when they treated the burning, nasty-looking scratch he'd received from the thing.

A feeling of unreality cloaked him, insulating him from thinking too closely about the encounter or his daddy's fate. In fact, his stomach grumbled. He noticed how the flesh on the young paramedic's cheeks jiggled. Like a bowl full of Jello. His stomach cramped with hunger.

At the hospital, the nursing staff offered him something to eat or drink.

"Yes, please." Billy's stomach growled louder, and somehow, he knew. He licked his chapped lips, pulled a strip off with his teeth, and savored the flavor of his own flesh. Yes, somehow Billy knew he'd never be able to eat enough to sate his rapidly growing hunger.

Yule Log

Joy breezed into her sister's home, kissing beside the cheeks of all she encountered. "Happy holiday!" She all but danced out of her winter coat, hand-knitted scarf, and mismatched gloves. "You beautiful souls!" She wrapped her sister-in-law, Hope, in another tight embrace, her many bangle bracelets clinking like music. "Thank you for hosting!"

Hope laughed and guided Joy into the living room. Two seven-foot-tall trees decorated with red ribbons, silver tinsel, and crystal bulbs stood on either side of an enormous, Victorian fireplace. From the marble and mahogany mantle, three white velvet stockings hung, each embroidered with the first initial of one of Hope's little children's names.

Said children, Nakita, Dimitris, and Eleni buzzed around the room, too excited to still themselves, despite their fussy dress clothes and the influx of impressive adults. They spotted their Aunt Joy at the same moment she spotted them. The four merged into a giggling mass of kisses and hugs.

"You've all grown so!" Joy's layered skirts engulfed them as completely as did her patchouli perfume when she sat on the floor to better adore her nieces and nephew. The four chattered and tumbled like playful kittens in a basket until the children were called away by the deep baritone of their father, Tom.

"Hello, Joy." He inclined his head but didn't make eye contact, opting instead to brush off his son's suit.

The doorbell announced another arrival, this one a cousin from Connecticut who presented the hosts a festively decorated wooden bough.

"It's a Yule Log. You burn it for luck." He chuckled, the twinkling lights from the Christmas trees reflecting off his thick glasses. He leaned conspiratorially to stage whisper to Tom, "I had this one made especially for you." He poked Tom in the center of his festive tie.

Tom stiffened and stepped away. "You don't say?"

"Oh, but I do," the Connecticut cousin answered before Tom placed the Yule Log, with its evergreen sprigs, false yellow flower, and red ribbon, on the hearth near the brass fireplace tools. With a look of distaste pulling his stoic mouth downward, Tom wiped his hands with a handkerchief found in his suit jacket.

Tom cleared his throat until every set of eyes save one turned to him. "It's nearly time for dinner. Please finish your cocktails and make your way into the dining room."

Tom retrieved his martini from a piecrust table, finished it, and proceeded to take his seat at the head of the table.

Joy studied the yule log, her face streaked with blushing color which somehow lent the appearance of a candy cane to her pale skin.

"Hello?" she whispered to the thing.

Before it answered, Hope asked, "Who are you talking to? And why are you still on the floor?" Hope giggled as she extended her hand and helped Joy to her feet.

Joy leaned in to whisper to her sister-in-law. "There's a spirit in that log."

Hope chuckled and rested her head against Joy's wild locks. "Honestly, it's no wonder Tom thinks you're odd." She guided Joy into the dining room, though Joy turned to look at the log over her shoulder.

The feast delighted the guests. After a salad and a tureen of roasted garlic soup, platters of roast goose, a dressed turkey, and a honeyed ham comprised the proteins. They passed baskets of rolls and butter molded into fanciful shapes. They scooped from crystal bowls filled with asparagus in hollandaise, brandied cranberries, seven bean salad, and three preparations of potatoes.

Joy ate only the vegetable dishes and the bread. Although the conversation buzzed around her, she found herself fascinated by the yule log brought from their Connecticut cousin, a man whose name she couldn't remember.

That cousin talked loudly at the far end of the table about his latest business venture. "You'd love the new shop, Joy," he announced around a mouthful of mashed potatoes and gravy. "I hired a couple of old hippies to stock it with all sorts of new age goodies."

Joy tipped her head to better view him. The Connecticut cousin's aura flickered an alarming dull red, brown, and black, a startling contrast to the contented oranges, greens, and pinks coming from Hope, the children, and most of the guests.

Joy wiped her mouth with a napkin before smiling at him. "Old hippies?"

He laughed. "Yeah, they're perfect for the shop. I keep them stocked with weed, and they almost work for free."

A woman Joy didn't know asked, "What sort of shop do you run?"

"It's a new age shop. They sell crystals and smudge sticks. Lots of books and native music. Dowsing rods and tarot cards. That sort of thing." He took a big bite of creamed cauliflower and spoke around it. "Profitable in that neck of New England."

"Well, that does sound right up your alley, doesn't it, Joy?" Tom emphasized the word 'your.'

Joy ignored her brother's implied sneer. "Smudge sticks and crystals are certainly helpful." She touched the quartz point hanging from a silver chain around her neck. "They offer ways to focus intentions. Clarity."

She turned again to the living room's hearth where the Yule Log rested. "Speaking of intentions," she caught the Connecticut cousin's attention. "What exactly were your intentions by bringing that log here?" Like her brother, she emphasized 'your.'

The cousin's round cheeks colored. He cleared his throat and tugged at his dark tie. "Intentions?" His guffaw silenced all other conversation. "Can't a man bring a present without having his motivations questioned?" His volume raised with the color of his cheeks.

Tom and Holly locked gazes in an "Oh dear" silent hosting alarm.

Tom cleared his throat, stood, and raised his stemmed wine glass. Bits of burgundy sloshed amiably therein, "Let's toast, shall we? To this season that brings together so many friends," he nodded to one side of the table, "and family." His nod to the other side was considerably briefer. He sipped his wine to a chorus of "here here's" and "well said's."

Hope clapped her hands. "Now for dessert!"

Pies of pumpkin custard, spiced apple and raisin, and coconut cream sat alongside imaginative cakes with icing crafted into holiday delights atop.

While everyone sipped piping hot coffees or teas with their choice of dessert, Joy whispered into Hope's ear. "Please, don't burn that Yule Log. Whatever you do."

Hope patted her sister-in-law's thin shoulder. "Don't worry, dear." Hope turned to prevent her son's acquisition of a third slice of festive cheesecake. "You'll upset your tummy. Now, say your good nights. It's well past your bedtime. You, too, girls." This last she directed to her daughters.

Joy kissed her nieces and nephew. She slipped silvered almonds into their palms with a wink. "Sleep with them under your pillow, and you'll dream of your future. Just don't forget, you must stay hopeful, unlike Phyllis."

The children giggled.

She continued. "You remember Phyllis, don't you?"

Nakita nodded. "You told us that story. She's the lady in ancient Greece who turned into an almond tree, right?" When Joy nodded, Nakita smiled, displaying pearly teeth. "See, we remember, Aunt Joy." All three nodded, and Joy kissed the tops of their heads. "You're such clever children!"

Tom's baritone rumbled, "Filling their heads with nonsense again?"

Joy cocked a crooked smile. "They're the same stories our folks told us."

"Bah. Myths." Tom pointed toward the bedrooms. "Off to bed, kids."

The three scampered up the stairs, waving hands fisted around their newest treasure to the other guests.

Tom turned to the adults and suggested after dinner drinks.

Hope giggled. "If I drink too much more, I'll float!"

Many of the guests chuckled. Some agreed with Hope. Others took Tom up on his offer. Joy leaned against a wall and watched the interactions, twirling a goblet of water between her palms.

The Connecticut cousin thumped a man in a black suit on his back, guffawing amiably. A third in their conversation joined the laughter, saying, "I do wish you wouldn't have to leave so soon."

"Can't be helped. It's a long trip back to Connecticut, you know."

All around the bedecked rooms, small groups came together and broke apart in an intricate societal dance, one Joy never quite understood but didn't tire of observing. She fell into a sort of trance, bewitched by the blending auras.

Her concentration broke, however, when someone's voice rose above the revelry.

"What a pretty fire! It really sets the mood."

From within the fireplace, the Yule Log crackled, its evergreen enhancements and ribbons steaming. As the bark peeled back, the spirit Joy had noticed burst from the wood. Gnarled joints like wood knots fisted, lips pulled back from wizened teeth, and malevolence gleamed in its ancient eyes. Its nostrils expanded, as though scenting prey.

The surprise caused Joy to drop her goblet. Water splashed into the thick pile of the carpet and onto nearby legs. Joy's airy voice wavered. "Oh, dear."

Another guest patted Joy's arm. "It's alright. It's only water. I'll grab a napkin."

The wood spirit burst from the fireplace with a gust of scorching sparks.

"Oh!" Hope and a small group of women stomped the singed spots on the carpet, passing near without noticing the spirit. The spirit tugged one of the women's braids, and she yelped, swatting her head.

She squealed, "Am I on fire?"

Hope and her companions spun the unfortunate lady, searching in vain for the cause of her distress.

Meanwhile, the wood spirit touched a wooden occasional table, and from its sanded sides sprouted twigs with tight, velvety buds. The wooden legs of the couch did the same, as did the hand carved elm sideboard.

Scorched pock marks on the carpet noted the spirit's passage. Somehow, though, the guests didn't seem to notice its presence. However, they did sidestep from its path, an unconscious self-preservation, and long-dead wood sprung to life as it brushed by. In a matter of minutes, the jovial assembly had become a fretful mob, bumping into one another without understanding what they avoided. They rushed for coats and hats, barely pronouncing their apologies before departing.

The wood of the furniture snaked toward the ceiling, snaring pant legs and skimming skirts. Smoke further complicated the vision when the wood spirit swelled tall as the ceiling, hunched over the decorated trees. Its bulk trapped the host and hostess who clung to one another, trembling, blinking at the chaos. Their frantic search skirted the spirit (which Joy realized must be invisible to the other guests) as they sought sense. Words shriveled behind the trembling lips of the normally loquacious couple. Their bewildered expressions begged for an end to, or at least an explanation for, the fantastic happenings in their normally peaceful home.

The spirit's body stretched until it hunched over the trapped couple. Its bulk threatened to engulf them. Offshoots from its center twisted around Tom's neck. His eyes widened, and gasping, he struggled against the unseen strangling. Hope found her voice and called her husband's name as a limb lifted her from her feet and dangled her near the fire.

Joy ran to the fireplace. She used the poker to roll the log and pounded it with the brass shovel until the fire extinguished.

Hope screamed, "Tom!" Her husband writhed on the floor, his face apoplectic. To her voice was added a chorus of concern from the children who had heeded the summons of commotion instead of the obligation of bedtime.

"Daddy!" They sprinted, unseeing, past the spirit and fell to their father's side.

"Spirit!" Joy raised her voice. "We meant no harm. Please stop this. You're killing him."

The spirit narrowed its eyes at Joy. "As you killed my brethren?" Offshoots from its body brushed along the wood in the room, drilling through plaster to find studs in the walls and ceiling support beams. Flooring and furniture and Christmas trees.

Joy's mind raced. "Please. Your wood provides our shelter. We bring in trees this time of year as a sort of kinship with nature. See how we decorate?"

Nakita blinked up at her Aunt Joy, and then following Joy's sightline stared at the enraged spirit. The child swallowed a scream, her hands flown to cover her gaping mouth. Somehow, she seemed to understand. She stayed on her knees and clasped her hands in front of her, orienting on the spirit. "Please, don't hurt my daddy."

Nakita's siblings noticed, and after their initial shock, joined Nakita's entreaty. Tears rolled over their young faces.

Joy reached toward the spirit's looming top. "Please." She removed her necklace and extended it to the being. The children reached into their robe pockets and offered whatever treasures they found therein. A thimble. Some wrapped candies. Coins. A few silvered almonds. A tiny doll.

The spirit shrunk. Its grip on Tom's throat released, and Tom gasped. Hope fell to the floor and ran to embrace him. He still gulped air. She was awash in tears.

The spirit snatched the offerings presented by Joy and the children, retrieved its one-time prison, the Yule log, and burst through one of the living room windows. Wintery, snow-rich air spiraled in its wake. The yellow, silk daisy that once decorated the Yule log danced like a tiny sun amid the sparkling white before it fell like a forgotten truth.

The children ran to their parents while Joy surveyed the damage.

When his voice returned, Tom struggled to his feet and asked, 'What the hell happened?"

"Do you remember the story of the Greek Horse?"

Tom all but growled. "I'm not in the mood for tall tales. What happened to my house?"

Joy picked up the false flower and shrugged. "You burned the Yule Log."

Hope gaped. "Your cousin said it was supposed to bring good luck!"

"He was always jealous of Tom, and he never specified the kind of luck, and…" Joy threw the flower into the fireplace's ash. "Not all luck is good."

"Oh Christmas Tree, Oh Christmas Tree, How Evergreen Your Branches!"

Creevy's Trees

An underlying stench of decay tickled his senses as Adam set the pine tree's trunk in the base. *I must be imagining things*, he thought, as he added water to hydrate the Christmas tree. His children, Bree and Chancey, hopped about with excitement as he set lights atop the prickling branches. "Ouch!" He plunged his thumb into his mouth to keep blood from speckling the carpet.

"Daddy's sucking his thumb!" Bree squealed.

Chancey set tiny fists on his hips. "Hey, I'm not allowed to do that. Why're you?"

Adam glared and resumed stringing the lights. Bree dropped a box, yielding the unmistakable sound of glass breaking. "Sorry, Daddy. It slipped."

"Where's your mother? She should be here for this fun family experience."

Bree stood taller. "She's shopping with Aunt Crystal. She said since she's done everything else around here, like cooking and cleaning and hanging all the other decorations and wrapping the presents, we should put up the tree."

"Shopping my ass," Adam muttered around another pricked finger. "Probably at the bar, sipping peppermint schnapps." He cleared a growing obstruction in his throat. His voice sounded strained as he said, "Garland, please." He stepped back. The red, white, and silver plastic garland made the pine look like a bizarre candy cane. "Does it look even?"

Bree clasped her hands beside her cheek. "It looks perfect."

He tousled the child's hair. "Glad you think so. Let's get the ornaments on before the game starts."

Chancey's finger ventured into his nostril. "Should we sing carols?"

"Dude, finger out of the nose. Sure, you can sing as you hang the ornaments." Adam threw away Bree's dropped box with its fragmented antique glass. He found a sparkling splinter in his wrist.

"Dang, decorating is dangerous."

The tree quivered as the kids hung ornaments as high as their reach allowed. Adam hung the pieces above their heads to even the display.

"Oh, Daddy, it's the beautifulest tree in the whole world! Where did you find it?"

Adam ducked his chin, wiping the back of his neck with a calloused hand. "Old lady Creevy's yard." Crazy bird kept enough trees on her acreage to stock a forest. She could do without this one.

Chancey thrust out his chest like a miniature detective, rocking on the balls of his feet. "I thought Mrs. Creevy said we couldn't buy any of her trees. She said they were important to her."

Bree tutted. "No, Chancey. She said they were sacred. Like at church, how the cross and stuff are sacred. It's nice that Mrs. Creevy changed her mind and let you buy one, Daddy."

Adam grunted. *Bought one? Yeah, that's it.* "Where's the star?"

"Right here!" Bree rushed to retrieve the box. Chancey raced her. The children collided, bloodying both noses.

He yelled over the kids' crying, "Great, you're going to look fabulous in pictures with your swollen noses. You best not have black eyes in the morning or your mom's going to kill me."

They elbowed each other as they rushed to the bathroom to staunch the blood flow.

An odd crackling like an old person's laugh drew his attention. Tree sap dripped from a spot on the trunk where a limb broke during transportation. He'd been in such a hurry to tie the thing to the top of his car and get away before the Creevy bat realized he cut the tree that in his haste, he snapped some limbs.

Christmas lights turned the amber sap crimson, then green, translucent, and fascinating as it formed an enlarging bulb. Another cackle sent chills through his spine. *Bet it's my wife playing a trick.*

"Not funny." he said, looking about. The merriment escalated, echoing through the room.

Don't think it's her.

Bree trembled in the hallway. Her eyes were wide over the bloodied hand towel she pressed to her nose.

"Daddy, what's that?"

Chills raced through his spine. *Not my imagination, then. She hears it, too.*

"Don't know." He waved her away. "You and your brother go to your rooms. Close the doors tight. I'll come get you soon."

She clung to the rag, tears dripping into a splatter-pattern that resembled a Santa hat. Her voice quavered. "Okay, Daddy."

The room reverberated with ear-shattering glee. Decay wafted through the room. Adam gagged.

From the enlarging pool of sap, a being formed. Pointed ears, an angular nose, and thrusting chin made a hideous caricature of "a right jolly old elf." Its face split into a smirk, displaying needle-sharp teeth.

"What the heck? Get out!"

It steepled its fingers together, the obscenely long claws clicking like breaking ice.

"Leave, Sonny? You brought me here."

It overturned the candelabra. Flames kindled in the fake evergreen garland, smoldering.

Adam reached to quench the fire. Sharp, hot pain followed by a thud, as his arm fell to the ground. He screamed and squeezed the stump. Sticky blood geysered from the wound. "What the fuck?"

The parody of a gnomish St. Nick licked its claws.

"Get out of my house!" Adam lunged at the thing, head lowered like an enraged bull.

It side-stepped, ragged red sleeve buffeting Adam as he careened past, stumbling to the ground.

Adam flipped over, feeble from blood-loss. His vision swam.

Its clawed toes scratched the hardwood, horrible grin mocking. Fire charred the wallpaper, and the smoke detector screeched. "Your family's tree needs a star."

His wife's voice interrupted. "Adam, what the hell's going on?"

The satanic Santa tipped its witchy chin. "Ah, a perfect tree topper!"

"No!" Adam lurched from the floor to tackle the thing as its nails flashed toward her head. Three bodies hit the floor. The room blurred, a blizzard of blood, and then blackness.

Adam struggled awake, strapped to a squeaking stretcher. An EMT's deep voice. "Domestic. Police'll arrest after he heals. Kids look beat up. Social worker has 'em."

A strangled scream caught in Adams' throat. His decapitated wife's wide-eyed horror stared from atop the tree, dripping gore like tinsel on the branches below.

"O Tannenbaum, O Tannenbaum…"

Secret Santa Helper

Instead of crisp, white snow, fog, and rain dampened Natalie Vance's lonely three block trek from her bus stop to her home. She jiggled the metal handle until she closed the latch on the battered, wooden pickets fencing in her small front yard. On the walkway, the rain had rinsed away her chalk drawings of Christmas trees and spindly-legged reindeer pulling Santa's red sleigh.

She had to be certain he knew where to find her, because Santa forgot to visit Natalie last year.

As the rain smeared her unevenly printed "Plez Come here, Mr. Santa" to pink and pale mint streaks, she stared at her undecorated house and concocted a plan. She could make some paper chains using red and green construction paper like she'd done in Mrs. Ellers' first grade class. Chin high and ponytails slicked to her cheeks, Natalie opened the front door to her house.

Or she would have, if the door was unlocked.

She hated it when her parents forgot to leave the door open for her. It was bad enough that she was the only first-grader whose parents didn't meet her when the bus doors opened on the corner of Ellis and Shady.

Natalie removed her backpack and sat on it, chin balanced atop balled fists, rain a steady nuisance. She glared up at the clouds and wished the awning hadn't blown off her house last spring, or that Daddy would have put it back on before Natalie had to sit, unprotected and locked out of her house. Again.

She flared her skirt out to cover her knees. She didn't mind sitting on the backpack, she supposed. It was old, and besides, she didn't have any "Santa's Secret Helper" presents in it that might be crushed.

The week before, Mrs. Ellers' class pulled names from a bright green elf hat with jingle bells on all of its white trimmed points. Natalie had pulled Samantha Bufford's name. Mrs. Ellers explained that the kids were to keep the names on their elf-hat notes a secret, which of course a lot of them didn't. But then, during the last week of school before winter break, they were allowed to bring a present to slip into the coat cubby of the kid whose name they pulled.

Mrs. Ellers explained that she'd put everyone's name in the jingly hat, so everyone would have a "Santa's Secret Helper" present, and "wasn't that nice?" But it wasn't nice. Not nice at all, because either her "Secret Santa's Helper" forgot to bring a present for Natalie, or Santa really had put Natalie on his "naughty list" and wouldn't even allow

Natalie a stupid present from the kid who pulled her name at school.

She'd used all of her piggy bank money to buy a story book box of all the kinds of Lifesaver candy ever made, wrapped it in aluminum foil because they didn't have wrapping paper, and taped to it Samantha Bufford's name that Natalie had pulled from the jingly elf's hat. Wasn't that something a "nice list" girl would do?

Natalie sniffed and wiped her streaming nose with the wet sleeve of her yellow Captain Cat hoodie. At least the rain disguised her "baby tears."

At the end of the school day, Natalie had leaned all the way into her cubby, hoping her "Santa's Secret Helper" had put her present way in the back where the shadows danced with spider webs and dust bunnies.

She was disappointed.

Randy Highmaker, a freckle-faced troublemaker from Natalie's class, witnessed Natalie's distress and guessed, "Nobody got Natalie a present!" His chant found echoes from others in the class, and Natalie's face blazed brighter than a yule log.

Natalie remembered yule logs. Her Pap used to cut apart their old Christmas trees, and Grandma would decorate a section to burn on the following New Year's Eve in the fireplace. Grandma's eyes sparkled when she explained, "It's a tradition, and burning the yule log reminds us something good can be made from everything, even a dried-up old tree."

Christmases were better before Grandma and Pap died. They knew the secret way of attracting Santa Claus. They must have forgotten to tell her parents, because with them gone, Natalie had nothing under the tree on Christmas morning.

Unless Natalie truly was naughtier than she realized.

A fire kindled and blazed through Natalie's insides. She no longer shook from the cold, but instead with an unfamiliar anger. It bubbled like the hard candy Grandma used to make with her, smelling of cinnamon and clear as glass until they added "just three" drops of food coloring, red as holly berries. It was Natalie's job to add the drops. She had stood on a chair beside Grandma, playing with the ribbon of the poinsettia apron around Grandma's plump waist.

Grandma always told Natalie she was a nice girl. So had Pap. Natalie's parents never told Natalie she was nice, though. They rarely said anything to Natalie at all, except to ask why she didn't clean up after herself or take out the garbage.

The bubbling internal heat boiled over. Natalie grabbed a rock and, with a high-pitched grunt, threw it at the living room window. Anger had given her strength, and Natalie's throw hit its mark. The glass shattered like the hard candy, jagged pieces tinkling from the window frame and crashing to the floor.

If Natalie's name were on the naughty list, maybe she should do something naughty.

Her feet kicked against the pale blue aluminum siding as she climbed through the new entry into her home. Her heart panged. Natalie really did a naughty something, and guilt wiggled into her belly. As she struggled to enter her house, a sharp piece of broken windowpane sliced into her palm. Natalie clamped her lips tight to keep from screaming from the pain. She heaved herself through and slid to the mess on the hardwood floor. More glass bit into her hands and crunched as she struggled to her feet. She'd clean this before her parents got home or she would be in big trouble.

"My, my, my."

Natalie spun at the sound, tinny, and gleeful.

A small, gnarled man perched on the windowsill, shaking his head. Soot smeared his skin, hair, and clothes until he better resembled a distorted shadow than any man Natalie had ever met. His lip quirked into a smile as crooked as his back. "You have made a mess, haven't you?"

Natalie nodded, wide-eyed with fright.

His gravelly voice demanded, "Go on then, Natalie, and clean up if that's your plan. You don't think I fancy getting all cut up, too, do you?"

Natalie shook her head and gulped, torn. She knew better than to talk to strangers, but this odd man knew her name. She didn't remember ever meeting him, but if he knew her, she must know him, too, right?

He gestured for her to run along, and she did. First, she put paper towels on her palms to stop the blood, and then she got a grocery store bag, the dustpan, and its dirty little whisk to brush up the mess. She half expected the strange man would be gone when she returned, but he still crouched in the corner of the window frame. The little broom and dustpan stung her tender palms and cut fingertips, and each pass streaked blood across the floor. Her blood.

The world spun a bit until the little man, smelling sharp and biting as flame, jumped to her side.

"Here now, you sit for a moment. I'll clean this up for you." He took a tiny broom made of white-barked branches and made quick work of the glass, then round-sat on the floor beside Natalie's drying blood. He stuck his finger into it and swirled the red around like finger paints.

"Was it a bad day?" He asked.

Natalie nodded. Tears dribbled over her cheeks and nose to join drops of her blood falling from her still-bleeding hands.

He licked his reddened fingertips and fixed her with a probing look. "Way I see it, you need a friendly ear. Mine's friendly. See?" He wiggled the tops, and Natalie giggled despite herself. "There's a good girl. Why not tell your Uncle Peter what's bothering you?"

Natalie didn't know she had an Uncle Peter, and despite his odd appearance, he had called her a good girl. She sniffed. "My Secret Santa Helper at school didn't give me a present, and mean old Randy Highmaker had got all of the kids in the class to laugh at me, and Mrs. Ellers said every kid would get a present, but I guess she didn't mean me, because I didn't and she didn't do anything about me not having one." When she was done, Natalie sobbed into the bloodied paper towels lining her palms.

"That is troubling." He crab-walked to her. "Let me see those hands of yours."

She sucked up her boogies and held out her hands.

He plopped the reddened paper towels into the bag with the glass, leaned close to Natalie's cuts, and picked out the remaining shards. "So, it sounds like your Secret Santa Helper should be on the "naughty" list."

Natalie sucked in her breath to keep from crying out as he pulled a long piece from her left thumb.

"And the kids in your class who laughed. They were naughty, too."

"Especially Randy Highmaker. He's the one who got the other kids to laugh at me."

"I see. I'm familiar with Master Highmaker." He chewed his bottom lip with yellowed teeth, intent upon a final piece of glass. "I don't suppose it will surprise you that he's been edging toward 'naughty' for some time."

Natalie's tears welled up.

"No, none of that. No crying. Here." He reached into an inner pocket of his jacket, dislodging a poof of ash as he did, and produced a gingerbread star with swirling white icing. "You munch on this while I take care of something. Is that okay with you?"

"I guess so." Natalie sniffed back snot bubbles. "What're you going to do?"

He shrugged. "My job." He bounced on his too-thin legs. "But there will need to be a payment."

Natalie gasped. "I don't have any money left in my piggy bank. I used it all to buy my Secret Santa Helper present."

"No, no, sweet girl. I wouldn't dream of taking your money." He lifted her hand as though he were a prince and she a princess. He brought her hand to his lips, palms up, and he licked her wounds.

Natalie gasped but couldn't pull her hand from his firm grip.

His tongue, rough as a cat's, circled her palm. He released her hand, pointed his sharp chin toward the ceiling, and closed his eyes. "Mmmmm, like candy." He sighed, then sprang up. "I'll be back soon." And quick as an ember sucked up a chimney, Peter disappeared.

Natalie visited the rusted medicine chest in the downstairs bathroom, but she found she no longer needed bandages on her left hand. Her cuts and scrapes had healed. However, she couldn't clean Peter's soot from her hands. She bandaged her right hand, dried her sodden hair, and trekked upstairs to change her wet and bloodied clothes.

When she made it downstairs, her father greeted her.

Or he would have, if he weren't beer-scented and blurry eyed and pointing at the broken window.

"What the hell did you do?"

When she didn't answer immediately, he shook her by her shoulders. "How many times do I have to tell you not to break my things?"

Natalie's head bounced like a rag doll's. "I'm sorry," she whimpered. "I didn't mean to."

He snatched at her hand. "Cut yourself, huh? Good! Maybe that'll teach you not to break other people's stuff." He squeezed until she cried. "Next time you get a stupid idea, think of how this feels." He pointed to the finger-painted flooring. "Clean that up before I get back."

"Where're you going, Daddy?"

"Never you mind where I'm going, but if your Mother ever gets here, tell her I've gone to Smitty's. I'm hungry."

Natalie's stomach growled. "Me, too," she whispered, but he never heard. The door closed behind him before she got the mop to clean what looked like a picture of Randy Highmaker being spanked by Uncle Peter.

The front door opened, and Natalie's mother sauntered in. "Hello, Natalie. Where's your Dad?"

"He said he was going to Smitty's."

"Oh, did he now? Well, I guess I'll just have to stop by and pick him up. Did he at least get you some dinner?"

Natalie stared at the floor beneath her mismatched socks and hoped her mother wouldn't notice the broken window. "No."

"You've got to be kidding me? Can you believe him?" Her mother stormed into the kitchen, complaining loudly, as she slapped peanut butter and jelly on bread. She didn't cut it into smaller triangles, the way Natalie liked. "Here. Eat this. Shit, you need something to drink."

"I can get some milk, Momma."

"Really? Okay. That would be a help."

"Can I get some for you, Momma?"

"No." She called from the bathroom where she brushed her hair and applied makeup. "I'm going to Smitty's to check on your father." She shrugged into her sparkly jean jacket and slipped her feet into high heels. "You eat your dinner and go to bed."

"Okay, Momma. Bye."

But her mother never heard as she rushed into the darkening evening.

"At least the rain stopped," Natalie supposed as she bit into her PB&J.

"It may snow later tonight." Peter's gravelly voice startled Natalie, and she dropped her sandwich on the floor. Instead of picking it up right away, she stared at it with a melancholy sigh.

"Now, little lady, I thought we agreed there would be no pouting."

"I thought we talked about crying."

Peter wagged a crooked finger at her and smiled, the edges of his lips curled with glee. "Smart girl! You're quite right, indeed." He took her right hand and peeled away the bandages, one by one. "Randy says he is sorry, by the way. Let's hope he's learned his lesson."

"Really, Randy said he's sorry? Wow! I don't think he's ever said he's sorry for anything, not even the time he broke all of the Kindergartener's macaroni necklaces."

Peter's right shoulder rose while his left dipped, an ill-shaped shrug. "We can only hope, for his sake." He produced his birch branch broom and tapped it against his leg. Soot eddied in the air and settled on Natalie's pant legs.

"So, I was thinking, I don't believe we can let Mrs. Ellers entirely off the hook. It was her job to be sure everyone participated in the Secret Santa Helper program. You brought in a gift, but nobody brought one for you."

It went against Natalie's nature to blame adults for anything, but she imitated Peter's lopsided shrug. "I guess so."

"Excellent." He licked her right palm with his overlong and rough tongue. Then, with a nod of his head, Peter disappeared.

Natalie cleaned the butter knife and jelly spoon her mother had used to make her spoiled sandwich. In the soap bubbles, she witnessed Peter's confrontation with Mrs. Ellis. Her teacher's eyes widened, bulged with terror, and Peter approached. He explained why she needed to be punished, but she ran. Peter scrambled after, his broom a stinging weapon. It slash, slash, slashed Mrs. Ellers along her arms, leaving brilliant red streaks bubbling with garnet and ruby blood. The bubbles popped with each of her screams.

Natalie rinsed the sink, dried the utensils, and put them away.

When she bent to throw away the ruined sandwich, she realized her legs were as sooty as Peter's, and no matter how much she rubbed them, the ash clung to her.

For the third time, Peter returned with delighted cackles. "Your teacher also apologized. Well, she did after a bit of persuasion."

Natalie studied his face. "What did you do to Mrs. Ellis?"

"I reminded her of the responsibility she undertook when she became a teacher. And now for my last task."

She held up her healed but sooty palms. "I don't have any more booboos. Thank you for making them better." She struggled to swallow. "Since I don't have any more boo-boo's, I don't think you can help me anymore." She furrowed her brows. "Besides, you talked to the people from school who made me sad. I think you're done."

"Dear girl, please don't worry. Be honest with me and with yourself. There's another task for this evening. Two naughties who need reminding of their responsibilities."

"But if I don't have any more boo-boo's, remember?"

He ran a hand twisted as tree roots along her cheek. "Agree to be my helper, and you'll be well taken care of."

"What would I have to do?"

"We teach lessons so people will remember to behave. We listen at chimney tops and scuttle down the flues to gather information. We spy through raven's eyes and learn what's inside the hearts of humans." He poked the end of her nose, and she knew she'd never again smell even the sweetest sugar cookies without first sniffing char.

"Do we get to see Santa?"

"Oh, yes, and we eat big feasts at the Claus's lovely table. You'll be enchanted, my dear, by their silvery-white reindeer. There's a long-faced donkey with whiskers white as time itself. He pastures with the Yule goats and three camels. There's a fashionable cat with eyes green as mistletoe, and invisible boys who get into mischief. And the elves!" He cackled. "They'll make you laugh sure as anything. There are trolls, too, and fairies light as sunbeams. And so many other delights. I can't wait for you to see them."

"Won't my parents be sad that I'm gone?"

Peter lowered his head as though he prayed, and she knew the answer.

Some instinct compelled her to ask, "But how will I pay?"

"You'll have to change your name." He smiled, and his teeth stood cracked and broken as the chimney pipes in an abandoned town. Still, she smiled back, excited to see the wonders of Christmas Land. It would be even better than being on the "nice" list, because she could live it every day.

"Get whichever toys you want to bring. I'll be back in two shakes of Jack Frost's head."

As she packed her favorite books, some treasured dolls, and her Teddy Freddy, Natalie imagined Peter visiting Smitty's. He'd waggle his twisted finger in her parents' faces, and when her father lunged, Peter would gambol out of his grip, his eyes alight with mischief. He'd dodge attack after attack until, with a red-faced effort, her father would fly across the bar to tackle Peter.

Natalie somehow knew what she imagined was real.

Peter stepped aside, sweeping his midnight robe like a matador baiting a bull. But her father didn't emerge from the other side. Her mother squeaked her distress, shaking hands to her trembling lips.

"No!" she said with more concern for her husband than she'd ever shown for Natalie. She also rushed the cockeyed little man, and like her husband, she disappeared into the inky eternity of his soot-infused cloak.

When he returned, Natalie grabbed the last thing for her bag. A photograph of her Grandparents. They had always told Natalie she was a good girl.

Natalie frowned at Peter "Will they ever get out of time out?"

"When your parents learn their lesson, they can come out."

"By the way, what's my new name?"

He smiled. "How about Hugin?"

Oogie Schemes

As the full moon slid into place on the brisk 26th of December, a gray shadow flitted across the ground. Those unfortunates nearby shivered and cast fearful, wide-eyed glances over their shoulders and hurried their steps. They wouldn't admit it, but their hearts beat a quickened childhood song that had nothing to do with Christmas joys but everything to do with remembered mischief. Even a saint mayn't turn a blind eye to every misdeed, after all.

They sped up steps, and when welcomed by friends and family, they spoke too loudly in the hopes of drowning the imagined chuckle of that old Boogieman that often-dogged people out alone after nightfall.

The shadow, in the meanwhile, scuttled to overturn rocks and collect the insects and arachnids found sleeping. The frozen ground entombed most of the bugs, though, and the search went frustratingly slow. Boogie gritted his incorporeal teeth and cursed the King of Halloween. If it weren't for Jack, Boogie would rule Halloweentown. He'd have made mincemeat of that old Sandy Claws and taken over Christmastown, too.

But Boogie wasn't confined to any of the holiday towns. No, not as long as there are children. He'd haunt their room and slither into their dreams any old day or night.

Disembodied giggles floated with wisps of snow. A snowball thumped through Oogie Boogie, and he growled. "Lock, Shock, and Barrel! Show yourselves!"

A claw-footed bathtub clattered across the frozen ground, bearing Halloweentown's favorite trick-or-treaters. Lock's squeaky voice piped up first. "Hello, Mr. Oogie Boogie, Sir!" He waved a devil-red hand.

Shock tilted her witchy head and smiled behind her witchy mask. "What can we do for you, oh Windy One?"

Barrel pushed his skull-masked face between the other two. "Hey, I wanted to ask!"

Shock pushed Barrel, and Lock thumped him on the head.

Before the three costumed characters could rumble further, a wind swirled around them, whipping bits of autumn debris in pumpkin spice spirals. The three paused, mid-punch, to listen to Oogie's baritone voice.

"Stop it this instant. Show me what you've got."

They shivered as they emptied their trick-or-treat sacks.

Oogie snatched up the insects they'd collected. Pill bugs and cockroaches, thousand leggers and beetles.

Oogie growled, low at first, then rising like a storm. "At last, enough!" Streetlights extinguished, plunging the area into inky darkness. Oogie gathered the miscreant minions and gave instructions that caused hairs to rise as gooseflesh.

"Right away, Oogie!" said Lock.

"We won't fail you, Mr. Boogie," said Shock.

Barrel saluted, "Sir."

The bathtub trundled off with the three scheming inside.

With a guttural laugh, Oogie Boogie set his spiders to spinning nets.

Maybe he wasn't as spry as the Pumpkin King or as lucky as Sandy Clause, but Oogie Boogie was clever and conniving. He'd head a holiday. All he had to do was capture that Baby New Year before its shiny ball reached the ground in Times Square. Then he, Oogie Boogie, would take over the role. He'd be the representation for the new year, and then, OH BOY, what fun that would be!

This of course is a tribute to Tim Burton's FABULOUS and beloved film "The Nightmare Before Christmas" and was written as a speculation for Michelle Halloween.

Acknowledgements

As ever, without the expert guidance of Debra Sanchez of Tree Shadow Press, this book wouldn't see the glowing lights of the holidays. (Thank you, Deb! You're a real blessing.)

My patient family, who endured take out, leftovers, and a messy house so I could put this together, also deserves my heartfelt thanks. I love you all more than I can convey!

The cover art by Christopher Blickenderfer from American Tattoo in Verona, Pennsylvania always wows. Thank you for sharing your time and talents!

And to God, Praise and Thanks Ever.

**A little something about songs. Music inspires and is inspired. Songs played in my mind during the crafting of several of these short tales, a background to set the mood as I organized my overactive thoughts. I've included a list of the muse for some of them, such as:

Valentine Toast – "Valentine" by Martina McBride

Sadie Hawkins – "Sadie Hawkins Dance" by Reliant K

Pam's Perfect Costume – "Devil in Disguise" by Elvis Presley

Bobbing Contest – "Better Metal Snake" by Dethklok

Buback – "Kiss of Death" by Doro Pesch of Warlock

Mrs. Kernel, Witch – "Season of the Witch" by Donovan

Nema – "Ghostbusters" by Ray Parker Jr.

Belinda's Blue Halloween – "Somebody's Watching Me" by Rockwell with Michael Jackson

Crossroads Inn – "Helloween" by Helloween

Classic Christmas Carols, too. Other stories have already proclaimed the inspiration in their titles. Did you guess the titles and artists?

Several of the works contained in this volume were first published in the following publications, though sometimes with different editing:

"Baby New Year" – *It's My Party*, Anthology, 2014

"Belinda's Blue Halloween" - *Frightful Tales for All Hallow's Eve*, 2015

"Benny the Beast" - *Spooky Halloween Drabbles*, 2014

"Betty Bumblebee" - *Jack-o'-Lanterns, 13 O'Clock Press*, 2016

"Beware the Ides of March" (renamed "Senator's Son") - *Dark Holidays Anthology, Dark Skull*, 2014

"Blakulla Hjalt" - *JEApers Creepers*, 2016; *Carousel of Nightmares*, 2018

"Buback" - *Michael's Parlor of Horror* first prize winner

"Egg Hunt" - *Speculative 66* issue 8

"Love and Porcelain" - *Carrot Ranch Literary Society*

"Mrs. Kernel the Witch" - *Jack-o'-lantern Tales of Treats & Tricks, FWG*, 2014

"O, Canada" - *Dark Holidays Anthology*, Dark Skull Publishing, 2014

"Oogie Schemes" - *Michelle Halloween*

"Pam's Perfect Costume" - Leg Iron Press *Halloween Anthology*, 2022

"Sadie Hawkins" - *Dark Holidays Anthology*, Dark Skull Publishing, 2014

"Stars in the Sand" - *Siren's Call* Zine, April, 2022

"Wakey Waysa" - *Speculative 66* issue 6

*For further reading, check out the above anthologies (There are some many cool stories, and anthologies are great ways to find new authors!), zines, and groups.

Other Works by the author:

Praise for *Herd of Nightmares*

(Winner of The Author Zone "TAZ" award as best anthology of 2020)

"Great collection displaying range from short- to gut-punch micro-fiction." *Five Stars - Michael Carter*

"...Chicken Noodle Soup for a Gothic Soul." *Five Stars - J. McAndrew*

"Kerry Black takes us on an adventure into the unexplained with every story and poem." *Five Stars - Naomi Raven*

"An amazing collection of short stories, poems & even haikus to make your imagination run wild!! A great addition to every library...highly recommend!" *Five Stars - Heidi, Amazon Reviewer*

Praise for *Fairy Herds and Mythscapes*

"If you're fascinated by fairytales and their re-tellings, do Not miss this one." *Five Stars - Swarup Biswas*

"With charm and originality, this book offers a delightful range of fairytales and myths that you'll want to read over again." *Five Stars - Tina, Amazon Reviewer*

"The author's cleverness comes into display through her well-woven plots and fascinating characters." *Four and a Half Stars - Eriha, Goodreads Reviewer*

Praise for *Carousel of Nightmares*

"Kerry Black offers an unexpected, expertly-written, scary and clever bag of dark goodies. I enjoy Kerry's prose and this is my favorite work of hers." *Five Stars - TMW*

"I highly recommend reading this collection of shorts, as well as anything else by Kerry E.B. Black…" *Five Stars - Chasity Nicole*

"I like Kerry E.B. Black's short stories. You never know where that wicked imagination will take you." *Five Stars - Caddynut29*

"A motley collection of dark fiction." *Four Stars - Michaelslxxii*

"Dark and creepy stories. I liked 'Animates' best. It was a fun book to read." *MmanJune10*

Praise for *Awakening at Equinox*
(Finalist in The Author Zone "TAZ" awards for Young Adult book 2021)

"I loved this writing. The flow was perfect, I didn't want to put it down." *Five Stars - Paul Preston*

"Great book!! Highly recommend!!" *Five Stars - Heidi, Amazon Reviewer*

Praise for *Spring of Spirits*

"This story is charming even though it deals with some heavy topics like suicide and mental illness. These characters are great and Casey truly is an angel." *Four Stars - Paul Preston*

Praise for *Poetic Nightmares*

(Finalist in The Author Zone "TAZ" awards in Poetry of 2023):

"Dark, personal, witty, and insightful poems. Kerry E.B. Black is a delicate blacksmith of poetry and with POETIC NIGHTMARES, it is your heart that lays on the anvil. Impactful phrases and chilling realizations take shape as Kerry uses her words as the hammer, pounding and pounding away..." – *Five stars - Paul Preston*

"*Poetic Nightmares* by Kerry E.B. Black invites readers to explore shadows in the moonlight as phantoms dance and melodies swirl during the witching hour. The poems come alive with intriguing descriptions—some dark and dreamy, and others more raw and visceral. It all combines to create a poignant collection that horror fans will immensely enjoy." ~ *Sara Tantlinger, Bram Stoker Award-winning author of The Devil's Dreamland*

About the Author

Kerry E.B. Black writes from a crowded, buttery colored cottage situated on the edge of a swamp outside of the city of Steel and Romero's Dead. Her collection of short scares, *Herd of Nightmares* won the 2020 TAZ Award. Her debut Young Adult novel *Awakening at Equinox* was a TAZ finalist in 2021, and her poetry collection *Poetic Nightmares* was a TAZ finalist in 2023. Kerry's a member of the HWA, Wily Writers, Nomadic Wordsters, and the College of Rough Writers. When she's not writing or trying to keep the house from slipping into the swamp, Kerry enjoys outings with her family and friends, travel, good food, taking tea, and of course reading all she can. This married mother of five (with two still at home; the rest have grown and spread their proverbial wings) is owned by three furry felines, Poe, Hemingway, and P.D. James, and she spends most of her Friday nights playing board games with her clever kiddos.

Please follow the author's social media for updates:
https://www.facebook.com/authorKerryE.B.Black/
https://twitter.com/BlackKerryblick
https://www.instagram.com/kerry_e_b_black/

About the Artist

Christopher R. Blickenderfer came into the world one Spring Equinox not so long ago (to some - but very long ago to others), his fists balled, his lungs engaged, and his white hair flying. He grew up in Penn Hills, a suburb of Pittsburgh, Pennsylvania, USA playing football in his neighborhood like his hometown NFL team the Steelers. He read comics and made nunchucks and grew to well over six feet four.

With two beautiful daughters and a son to inspire him, Chris makes a living owning and running what is possibly the best Tattoo Shoppe in the known world, which if you've seen some of the tattoo shops around the world, you'd know how impressive that statement truly is. His shop is named American Tattoo, and it is located in Verona, Pennsylvania, USA, which is a little town with the distinction of having one of the shortest intersections in the nation. Chris, sometimes called "Blick," regularly wins awards for his beautiful artwork using any medium.

Chris doesn't have as much social media presence as he should, which is something he really should remedy, but he can be reached by email at:
americantattoo741@gmail.com .

www.ingramcontent.com/pod-product-compliance
Lightning Source LLC
Chambersburg PA
CBHW070821180626
46818CB00001B/356